Travel, English, and Fun!

說著英語

去旅行 二版

Beach
Hotel
BAR

MP3

Carlos Campbell — 著
Cosmos Language Workshop — 譯
Judy Majewski — 審訂

CONTENTS

1 訂機票／出境
BOOKING FLIGHTS / DEPARTURE

DIALOGUE 1
Confirm Reservation 確認訂位 (001)

A Hello. I'd like to confirm my reservation.
My name is Anne Lin.

B What's your name again, please?

A L-I-N, Lin.

B I see. What's your flight number?

A I'm on Flight 724 to London on October 31.

B Hold on, please   . Yes, Flight 724 for London,
departing on October 31, is confirmed.

A 喂，我叫林安妮，我想再確認之前的訂位。

B 麻煩您再說一次您的姓氏。

A L-I-N，林。

B 了解。請問您是搭哪一個班次？

A 10月31日到倫敦的724號班機。

B 請您稍候一下……您預訂10月31日飛往倫敦的
724號班機，已經幫您確認好了。

Study Points

I'd like to . . .	我想……	這是比較禮貌的説法，意思是「I want to . . .」。
flight number	飛機班次	每個航班都按一定規律編訂號碼，以便於區別和管理。
on flight 724	搭乘 724 號班機	搭乘飛機，介系詞要用 on。
hold on	稍等，不要掛斷	這是電話常用語。
depart	出發；離境	相對用法是 arrive（抵達）。

機票行程常用語彙

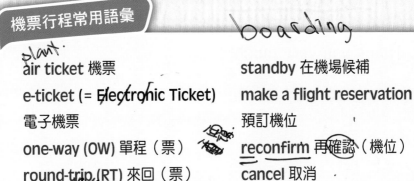

boarding

plant.
air ticket 機票

standby 在機場候補

e-ticket (= Electronic Ticket)
電子機票

make a flight reservation
預訂機位

one-way (OW) 單程（票）

reconfirm 再確認（機位）

round-trip (RT) 來回（票）

cancel 取消

circle trip (CT) 環遊票（機票）

status （訂位）狀況

round-the-world (RTW)
環球行程（機票）

states.

AIRLINE TICKET ✈

ECONOMY   BOARL

PASSENGER TICKET AND BAGGAGE CHECK
NAME OF PASSANGER
SURNAME / NAME

FLIGHT
GH 9124

DATE
23 MAY

ZONE
A

NAME OF PAS
SURNAME

FROM: DOLOR CITY
CONSECTETUR

GATE
A27

SEAT
19E

TIME
19E

FROM: DOLO
TO: CONSE

TO: DOLOR

NAME OF PASSANGER
SURNAM

BOARDING
17:20

AA00123456 897 37

GATE CLOSES 25 MINUTES BEFORE DEPARTURE

FLIGHT
GH 9124

D

GATE
A27

SEAT
19E

TIME
19E

AA00123456 897 37

Airline
TICKETS

BUY NOW

Checking In 辦理登機手續 002

A I'd like to check in.

B May I have your ticket and passport, please?

A Here you are. I'd like a window seat.

B No problem. Put your baggage on the scale, please.

A All right.

B OK. Here's your ticket, boarding pass, passport and baggage claim tag. You'll be boarding at Gate 8. The boarding time is 9 a.m.

A Thank you very much.

A 我要辦理登機手續。

B 請給我您的機票和護照。

A 在這裡。我想要靠窗的座位。

B 沒問題。請把行李放在磅秤上。

A 好。

B 可以了。這是您的機票、登機證、護照和行李提領證。您的登機時間是早上9點，請由8號登機門登機。

A 非常謝謝你。

Study Points

May I have your . . . ?	可以給我您的……嗎？	當地勤人員向你要東西時，會用此說法。
Here you are.	在這裡／給你。	當遞交東西給對方時的用語。
put . . . on . . .	將……放在……上	「put . . . under . . .」是「將……放在……下」。
Here's your	這是您的……	若東西為複數，則為「Here are your . . . .」。
board	登機	boarding gate 為登機門；boarding time 為登機時間。

TRAVEL CLASS 客艙級別

代號	級別	說明
F Class	頭等艙	First Class
C Class J Class	商務艙	Executive Class Business Class Dynasty Class
Y Class	經濟艙	Economy Class

不同的艙等（class），有不同的「票價等級」（fare basis）。按國際航空票務規定，經濟艙有 Y、B、M、Q、V、H、L 等七個不同的票價等級。Y 是經濟艙票價等級中的全價票，上述七個艙等中字母越接近左邊（Y）的，表示票價折扣越少；反之，越接近最右邊（L）的，表示票價折扣越多，機票的限制也越多。

DIALOGUE 3
Going Through the E-gate 自動查驗通關

Ⓐ Shouldn't we be going this way to passport control?

Ⓑ Let's go through the e-gates.

Ⓐ E-gates? I've never done that.

Ⓑ Come on, I'll show you. It's easy. Lots of airports have them now.

Ⓐ What do I need to do to go through an e-gate?

Ⓑ Just let the machine scan your passport and then look at the monitor. At some airports, I think you need to leave your fingerprints.

Ⓐ Sounds very convenient!

Ⓐ 我們不是應該走這邊去護照查驗處嗎？

Ⓑ 我們去走自動查驗通關吧。

Ⓐ 自動查驗通關？我從來沒使用過。

Ⓑ 來吧，我來教你，這個很簡單，
現在很多機場都有。

Ⓐ 走自動查驗通關應該怎麼做呢？

Ⓑ 只要讓機器掃描你的護照，然後看向螢幕。
有些機場還需要留下你的指紋紀錄。

Ⓐ 聽起來好方便！

Study Points

Shouldn't we . . . ?	我們不是應該…… 嗎？	相反説法為「Should we . . . ?」（我們應該……嗎？）。
go through	穿過；穿越	穿越某物的介系詞要用 through。
lots of	很多	等同於 a lot of。
What do I need to do . . . ?	我需要怎麼做才 能……？	詢問做某事應該要怎麼做的問法。
Sounds very convenient!	聽起來很方便！	「聽起來很……」都能使用此句型，如 Sounds very easy!（聽起來很簡單！）。

台灣申辦自動查驗通關辦法：

■申辦資格：
　1. 年滿 14 歲、身高 140cm 以上。
　2. 未受禁止出國處分之有戶籍國民。

■申辦文件：護照、身分證（或駕照、健保卡）／ 居留證。

■申辦地點：機場、移民署服務站、外交部領事事務局
　　　　　　（詳細地點請上網查閱）。

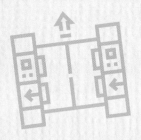

e-Gate 自動查驗通關閘門

1 **air ticket** 機票

2 **airlines** 航空公司

3 **electronic ticket** 電子票

4 **flight itinerary** 班機行程

5 **flight number** 飛機班次

6 **reserve** (v.)
reservation (n.) 訂位

7 **confirm** (v.)
confirmation (n.) 確認

8 **cancel** (v.)
cancellation (n.) 取消

9 **flight connection** 轉機

10 **transfer** 不同航班的轉機

11 **transit** 原機過境

12 **first class** 頭等艙

13 **business class** 商務艙

14 **economy class** 經濟艙

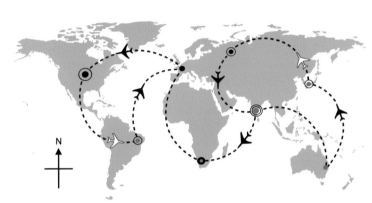

15 **airline code** 航空公司班機代號

16 **airport code** 機場縮寫

17 **city code** 城市縮寫

18 **origin** 起站

19 **destination** 終站

20 **stopover** 停留站

轉機方式

轉機（flight connection）的方式有三種：

1. 不同航班的轉機（**transfer**）：轉機的旅客在轉機點（**stopover point**）下機後，要遵循「**Transfer**」的標示走到轉機櫃台辦理報到，改搭另一班飛機。

2. 同航班的中途過境（**transit**）：同一架飛機在途中降落，讓到站的旅客下機，或是讓新搭的旅客上機，而中途不下機的旅客則在飛機上或機場等候起飛。

3. 隔夜轉機（**stopover night**）：旅客無法在同一天轉機到目的地時，航空公司會提供免費住宿，讓旅客隔天再改搭別的飛機。

DEPARTURE
PROCEDURE
出境流程

CHECK-IN COUNTER
**到航空公司的劃位櫃檯
辦理報到手續**

1

搭機時,要往 **Departure**(出境)走,
不要走到 **Arrival**(入境),然後到所搭
乘的航空公司的**劃位櫃檯**(**Check-
In Counter**),
辦理報到。現在
也有許多航空
公司設有**自助
報到機台**(**Self-
Service Check
-In**),旅客可先
自行辦理自動報
到取得登機證,
再前往劃位櫃台進行驗票。

驗票→**託運行李過磅**(weigh)
→**貼行李標籤**(claim tag)

行李若超重,須支付**超重運費**
(overweight charge / excess
baggage charge)。每家航空公司
對**託運行李**(checked baggage)與
手提行李(carry-on baggage / hand
baggage)限制的件數與重量不盡相同,
建議事先查好所搭乘的航空公司規定。

2

如果想選擇座位,可於此時提出詢問:
→**靠窗座位**:Window Seat
→**靠走道座位**:Aisle Seat
→**中間座位**:Middle Seat

若是個人購買機票、而非團體票,通常
在訂位時即可預選位子劃位(**book a
seat**),在報到時若想更換位子,也只
能針對尚空著的位子做更換。每間航空
公司的開票時間不定,有時也跟機票價
格與艙等有關,建議在訂票時即詢問清
楚,免得發生無法選位或必須跟同伴分
開坐的情形。

3

領取**登機證**（**boarding pass**）及**行李標籤**（**claim tag**）。登機證上會記載你的：
→ **飛機班次**：Flight No.
→ **登機門**：Boarding Gate No.
→ **登機時間**：Boarding Time
→ **座號**：Seat No.

4

依機場規定購買**機場稅**（**airport tax**）
（我國機場稅已內含在機票中）

B

PASSPORT INSPECTION AREA/ PASSPORT COUNTER
護照查驗

將護照及登機證等備妥，接受查驗。

現在各國的國際機場也設置了**自動查驗通關系統**（**e-Gate**），只要事先完成自動通關申辦，以後在出入境時就能省去排隊的時間，加快通關速度。

e-Gate 自動查驗通關系統

C

PASSENGER AND BAGGAGE INSPECTION
旅客及隨身行李檢查

此處分為人走的**金屬探測器**（**metal detector**），及隨身行李和物品走的**行李X光**（**baggage X-ray**）兩項檢查裝置。

metal detector 金屬探測器

baggage X-ray 行李X光

BOARDING GATE
前往登機門

1

登機證（boarding pass）上會註明登機門號碼與登機時間，接著依指示前往登機門。此時可利用時間上廁所，或到美食部、免稅商品店逛逛。

boarding pass 登機證

登機門號碼

登機時間

boarding gate 登機門

2

在登機前半小時到**候機室**（**lounge**）等候。

lounge 候機室

BOARDING
登機

聽到登機廣播後，拿出登機證以供服務人員查驗並登機。

board the plane 登機

出境攜帶物品限制
Baggage Policy
& Restrictions

託運行李禁止品項
What NOT to pack
in your checked baggage

■ 行動電源（power bank）、鋰電池（lithium battery）／含有鋰電池的電子產品：須放置隨身行李，因鋰電池在溫度與壓力變化劇烈的情況下，有膨脹甚至是起火爆炸的風險。

■ 打火機（lighter）：須隨身攜帶，且每人限帶一個傳統型打火機。

■ 高壓式噴瓶（high pressure sprayer bottle）：有些噴霧為高壓式噴瓶（如髮膠），在行李艙有爆炸的危險。

隨身行李禁止品項
What NOT to pack
in your carry-on baggage

■ 各式刀剪類或尖銳物品：各種刀剪，如剪刀、美工刀、修眉刀、指甲剪等；或是如開罐器、圓規等鋒利物品，一律禁止攜帶上機。

■ 超過 100 毫升的液體：不得攜帶超過 100 毫升（100 c.c.）的液體上機（註：安全考量，因任何不超過100毫升的液體危害性極小），且所有裝有液體、膠狀或噴霧類的瓶罐須裝在不超過一公升（1000 c.c.）的可重複密封之透明夾鏈袋中。

■ 收合後超過 60 公分的自拍桿（selfie stick）／超過 60 公分的腳架（tripod）：管徑超過 1 公分、且長度超過 60 公分的自拍桿或腳架，因具有攻擊性也禁止攜帶上機。

1 訂機位

❶ I'd like to book a flight from Hong Kong to Chicago on Tuesday, July 12.
我要訂7月12日星期二從香港飛芝加哥的機票一張。

❷ I'd like to book a flight that leaves in the morning.
我要訂一張早上出發的機票。

❸ I'd like to reserve a seat for Boston on May 8.
我想訂一張5月8日去波士頓的機票。

❹ I'd like to reserve a seat from Los Angeles to Taiwan.
我想訂一張從洛杉磯到台灣的機票。

SENTENCE PATTERNS 基本句型

出發地　　目的地　　　時間

I'd like to book a flight from Vienna to Seoul on Sunday, July 1.

我要訂一張在時間從出發地飛往目的地的機票。

目的地　　　時間

Are there any flights to Frankfurt on August 7?

有在時間飛往目的地的機票嗎？

機票常用語彙

normal fare 普通票價

full fare (adult fare) 全票（12 歲以上）

half fare (children's fare) 半票（2 至 12 歲，票價為全票的一半）

infant fare 嬰兒票（2 歲以下，票價為全票的 1/10，無座位）

fully booked 客滿

overbooking 超額訂位

5 Are there any flights to Beijing on Sunday?

有星期天飛往北京的機票嗎？

6 Are there any direct flights to Vancouver?

有沒有直飛溫哥華的班機？

7 What time does Flight 724 arrive in Singapore?

724號班機幾點會到新加坡？

8 Which airport do I leave from?

我要去哪一個機場搭機呢？

9 How much is the airfare from Paris to Taipei?

從巴黎到台北的機票是多少錢？

10　Ⓐ　When would you like to leave?

　　Ⓑ　① I'd like a flight on May 15.

　　　　② The sooner, the better.

　　Ⓐ　您要什麼時候出發？

　　Ⓑ　① 我要5月15日出發的班次。

　　　　② 可以的話，越早越好。

⑪ May I confirm my reservation? 我可以確認訂位嗎？

---

⑫ Please confirm my flight. 請幫我確認之前訂的機位。

---

⑬ May I have your name and flight number?
請告訴我您的姓名和搭乘的班機號碼。

---

⑭

Ⓐ Your name, please.

Ⓑ Lily Wu. Wu is my family name.

Ⓐ How do you spell it?

Ⓑ That's W-U, Wu.

Ⓐ I can't find your name on the list.

Ⓑ I made my reservation in Taiwan.
Would you check it again, please?

Ⓐ 麻煩告訴我您的大名。

Ⓑ 我叫吳莉莉，吳是姓氏。

Ⓐ 怎麼拼呢？

Ⓑ W-U，吳。

Ⓐ 名單上沒有您的名字耶。

Ⓑ 我是在台灣訂位的，請您再查查看。

---

⑮ My name is David Lee. My flight number is BA604 to Sydney
on October 2.
我的名字是李大衛，我的班機是10月2日飛往雪梨的BA604號。

---

⑯ I'd like to confirm the departure time. 我想確認起飛的時間。

---

⑰ By what time should I check in? 我幾點前要辦好登機手續？

18 I'd like to change my reservation. 我想改班次。

19 I'd like to change my flight date from June 5 to June 9.
我想把6月5日的班機改為6月9日。

20 I'd like to change a reservation for flight number 212 on March 22. 我想改3月22日212號班機的訂位。

21 Can I change my reservation to an earlier flight?
我可以改搭早一點的班機嗎？

22 Which flights have seats available? 哪一個班機還有位子？

23 I'll go standby. 我要排候補。

landing 降落　　　takeoff 起飛　　　runways 機場跑道

control tower 塔台

apron 停機坪

jet bridge;
passenger walkway 空橋

3 在機場辦理登機手續

24 I'd like to check in now. 我現在想辦理登機手續。

25 Please show me the seating plan. 請讓我看座位表。

26 I'd like a window seat, please. 請給我靠窗的位子。

27 I'd like an aisle seat, please. 請給我靠走道的位子。

28 A seat somewhere in the front, please. 請給我前面的位子。

29 A seat somewhere in the back, please. 請給我後面的位子。

30 I'd like to sit with my friend. 我要和我的朋友坐在一起。

31 Altogether I have two pieces of luggage. 我一共有兩件行李。

32 I'd like to bring this on board. 我這個是要帶進飛機上的。

33
- Ⓐ Your baggage is overweight. 您的行李超重了。
- Ⓑ How much is the extra fare? 那超重要付多少錢？

34 What is the boarding time? 登機時間是什麼時候？

35 Where is the boarding gate? 登機門在哪裡？

36 What is the gate number for the United Airlines flight to Rome? 聯合航空飛往羅馬的登機門是幾號？

37 Is this the right way to Gate 14? 14號登機門是往這裡走嗎？

38 Where is the duty-free shop? 免稅店在哪裡？

4 通關安檢與登機

39 Please walk through the security gate.
請通過安檢門。

40 Please open your bag. We'd like to have a look.
請把您的包包打開，我們要檢查一下。

41 Just make sure you don't have any liquid with you.
我只是要確定您沒有攜帶液體。

42 Test again. 行李再過一次X光機。

43
　A When is the boarding time?
　　什麼時候可以登機？
　B I'm afraid your flight is delayed.
　　您的班機可能誤點了。

44 May I have your attention, please. Thai Airlines flight TG 635 to Bangkok is now boarding. Passengers in the first class, please proceed to the boarding gate now.
各位旅客請注意，飛往曼谷的泰航TG635班機，已經開始登機，請頭等艙的旅客前往登機門。

45 Attention, please. Due to weather conditions, all flights to Taipei will be delayed. We truly regret the delay. Thank you for your cooperation and patience. We will inform you of the new departure time as soon as possible. Thank you.

各位旅客請注意，由於天候不佳，所有飛往台北的班機都將延後起飛。我們對此深表歉意，並感謝您的配合與耐心。我們將盡快通知您班機新的起飛時間，謝謝。

5 廉價航空

46
A May I upgrade to first class?
我可以升等至頭等艙嗎？

B I'm sorry. Only economy class seats are available on this flight.
很抱歉，此班班機只有經濟艙座位。

47
A Will you be serving a meal on this flight?
這班班機有供餐嗎？

B As we're a budget airline, we don't serve free meals on our flights.
由於我們是廉價航空，所以機上不提供免費餐點。

48
A Will there be complimentary drinks and snacks?
你們會提供免費的飲料和點心嗎？

B Drinks and snacks are available, but you'll have to pay extra for them. 我們有提供飲料和點心，但需要額外付費。

AT THE AIRPORT 來到機場

Airport 機場

Shuttle Bus 接駁車

Domestic Terminal 國內線航廈

International Terminal 國際線航廈

Cargo Terminal 貨運站

Arrival Lobby 入境大廳

Departure Lobby 出境大廳

Transit Room 過境室

Connection Counter 轉機櫃檯

Transfer Desk 轉機櫃檯

Information Counter 服務台

Courtesy Room; VIP Lounges 貴賓室

Waiting Room 候機室

Duty-free Shop 免稅商店

Check-in Counter 報到櫃檯

Luggage Scale 磅秤

Baggage Tag 行李牌

Carry-on Baggage 隨身攜帶的行李

Trolley 手推行李車

Security Check 安全檢查

Immigration Office 入出境辦公室

Customs Service Counter 海關服務櫃檯

Animal & Plant Quarantine 動植物檢疫

✈ Departures

Time	To	Flight no.	Gate	Remarks
09:35	NEW YORK	DF 2753	A1	DEPARTED
09:40	FRANKFURT	LN 3211	C3	BOARDING
09:45	TORONTO	GT 4638	A2	DEPARTED
09:45	LONDON	KV 3323	B4	ON TIME
09:50	MIAMI	LX 3100	A2	DELAYED
09:55	SYDNEY	LV 2317	A5	ON TIME
10:00	PARIS	BD 9032	B1	ON TIME
10:00	OSLO	FB 5610	C4	ON TIME
10:05	HONG KONG	EN 4267	A4	DELAYED
10:10	BARCELONA	GC 5433	C1	ON TIME
10:15	TOKYO	LY 4488	B2	ON TIME
10:20	MOSCOW	KF 3280	B4	CANCELLED
10:25	ZURICH	TK 7252	A4	ON TIME
10:30	LOS ANGELES	TK 3946	A1	ON TIME
10:35	ROME	RZ 1408	B3	DELAYED
10:40	HONOLULU	EK 4319	A1	NEW TIME

班機出發時間表
Departure Board

① **Departure Board** 班機起飛時間表
② **Take-Off Time** 起飛時間
③ **Destination** 目的地
④ **Airline Code** 航空代碼
⑤ **Flight Number** 班機號碼
⑥ **Boarding Gate** 登機門
⑦ **Remarks** 備註

⑧ **Departed** 已起飛
⑨ **Boarding** 登機中
⑩ **On Time** 準時
⑪ **Delayed** 誤點
⑫ **Cancelled** 取消
⑬ **New Departure Time** 已更改時間

有些機場的 departure board 會標示
SCHED-TIME（scheduled-time 預訂起飛時間）和
EST-TIME（established-time 實際起飛時間）。

備註欄的班機狀態還有可能出現下列訊息：

★ FINAL CALL 最後登機廣播
★ CHECK-IN NOW 辦理登機手續中
★ TIME CHANGE 時間更改

時刻表用語

Departure Board 起飛時刻表
Arrival Board 抵達時刻表
Estimated Time of Arrival (ETA) 預定抵達時間
Estimated Time of Departure (ETD) 預定起飛時間

登機證 Boarding Pass

BOARDING PASS ✈ Air Company

④ ECONOMY

① NAME OF PASSENGER
SMITH / JOHN
② FROM: MOSCOW   / DME
TO: LARNAKA   / LCA
③ FLIGHT
OKL018
DATE
12 NOV 2015
⑤ GATE   ⑥ BOARDING TIME
47   **11:30**

ETKT 5552115239450   ⑦ SEAT
24A

HAVE A NICE TRIP!

① **Name of Passenger** 旅客姓名
② **From . . . to . . .** 出發地與目的地
③ **Flight Number** 班機號碼
④ **Class** 座艙等級
⑤ **Gate Number** 登機門號碼
⑥ **Boarding Time** 登機時間
⑦ **Seat Number** 座位號碼

Departure
出境

Arrival
入境

Information
Center 詢問處

Customs
海關

Waiting Room
候機室

Pass
通關

Airport
Terminal
航廈

Passport
Control
護照檢查

Baggage
Scanning
行李掃瞄

Weighing of
Luggage
行李過磅

Ticket
Checking
機票檢查

Control Tower
塔台

X-ray
Scanning
機場 X 光檢查

Locker
寄物櫃

Duty-free
Shop
免稅商店

AIRPLANE
E-TICKET
電子機票
中英對照

```
                    ELECTRONIC TICKET
                PASSENGER ITINERARY/RECEIPT
                    CUSTOMER COPY
```

① Passenger: LI, MEI-HUEI   **④** Ticket No: 0015704034215
② Booking Ref: MFEGXF   **⑤** Issuing Airline: AMERICAN AIRLINES, INC.
③ Frequent Flyer No: **⑥** Tour Code: AATWAO

⑦ DATE		**⑧** CITY/STOPOVER	**⑨** TIME	**⑩** FLY/CLS/ST	**⑪** EQP/FLY TIME	**⑫** FARE BASIS
15AUG	DEP	TAIPEI TAOYUAN, TPE	1000	JL802	NON-STOP	YNE08YNO/
		TERMINAL 2		ECONOMY (Y)	788	TWO2
15AUG	ARR	TOKYO NARITA	1420	OK	03HR20MIN	
		TERMINAL 2				

⑬ OPERATED BY JAPAN AIRLINES/JAPAN AIRLINES INTERNATIONAL COMPANY LTD

JAPAN AIRLINES REF:6FBQXK			SEAT:		NVA:15AUG17	BAG:2PC
15AUG	DEP	TOKYO NARITA	1830	AA60	NON-STOP	YNE08YNO/
		TERMINAL 2		ECONOMY (Y)	BOEING 777-200	TWO2
15AUG	ARR	DALLAS INTL	1630	OK	12HR00MIN	
		TERMINAL D				

⑭ OPERATED BY AMERICAN AIRLINES/AMERICAN AIRLINES, INC.

❶ **Passenger Name** 旅客姓名
   拼法必須與護照姓名相同，否則無法登機，因此機票不可轉讓。

❷ **Booking Reference Number** 預訂代碼

❸ **Frequent Flyer Number** 飛行常客號碼

❹ **E-Ticket Number** 電子機票號碼

❺ **Issuing Airline** 核發航空

❻ **Tour Code** 團體代號：用於團體機票

❼ **Date** 出發日期

❽ **City** 出發與目的城市 / **Stopover** 中途停留

❾ **Time** 出發時間

❿ **FLY (flight number)** 航班號碼 / **CLS (class)** 艙等 / **ST (status)** 狀態

⓫ **EQP (equipment)** 班機型號 / **FLY Time (flying time)** 飛行時間

⓬ **Fare Basis Code** 票種代碼

⓭ **The airline that takes passengers to the stopover**
   載旅客前往中途停留點的航空公司

⓮ **The airline that takes passengers to the destination**
   載旅客前往目的地的航空公司

Airlines

YOUR TICKET-ITINERARY

YOUR BOOKING NUMBER : | WXIKXI

Flight	From		To		Aircraft	Class/Status
WK 2200	Montreal-Trudeau (YUL) Thu May-04-2019	17:15	Frankfurt (FRA) Fri May-05-2019	06:30+1	333	Y Confirmed
WK 2495	Frankfurt (FRA) T1 Fri May-05-2019	07:50	Amsterdam (AMS) Fri May-05-2019	09:00	321	Y Confirmed
WK 2293	Munich (MUC) T2 Mon May-22-2019	15:30	Montreal-Trudeau (YUL) Mon May-22-2019	17:50	340	Y Confirmed

Passenger Name	Ticket Number	Frequent Flyer Number	Special Needs
(1) JONES, JOHN/MR.	012-3456-789012	000-123-456	Meal: VGML

Purchase Description	Price	
Fare (LLXSOAR, LLXGSOAR)	CAD	558.00
Canada - Airport Improvement Fee		15.00
Canada - Security Duty		17.00
Canada - GST #1234-5678		1.05
Canada - QST #12345-678-901		1.20
Germany - Airport Security Tax		18.38
Germany - Airport Service Fees		37.76
Fuel Surcharge		161.00
Total Base Fare (per passenger)		809.39
Number of Passengers		1
TOTAL FARE	CAD	809.39

Ticket is non-endorsable, non-refundable
Changes allowed, subject to availability,
no later than 2 hours before departure.
Please read carefully all fare restrictions.

Have a pleasant flight!

Paid by Credit Card XXXX-XXXX-XXXX-1234

(cc by Airodyssey)

❶ **Booking Number** 預訂代碼
❷ **Flight Number** 航班號碼
❸ **From . . . To . . .** 出發地與目的地
❹ **Aircraft Type** 班機型號
❺ **Airline Class** 航班艙等
❻ **Seat Status** 座位狀態
❼ **Time** 出發時間
❽ **Passenger Name** 旅客姓名
❾ **Ticket Number** 機票號碼
❿ **Frequent Flyer Number** 飛行常客號碼
⓫ **Special Needs** 特殊需求
⓬ **Purchase Description** 購買細節
⓭ **Price** 價格
⓮ **Total Fare** 總額
⓯ **Forms of Payment** 付款方式

Visa 簽證
Visa on arrival 落地簽證
Visa-free 免簽證

1 **Issuing Post Name**
簽證核發地

2 **Control Number** 簽證號碼

3 **Surname** 姓

4 **Given Name** 名

5 **Visa Type** 簽證種類
Regular 一般
Official 公務
Diplomatic 外交
Other 其他

6 **Class** 艙等

7 **Passport Number** 護照號碼

8 **Sex** 性別
M (male) 男 / F (female) 女

9 **Birth Date** 生日

10 **Nationality** 國籍

11 **Entries** 入境次數
M (multiple) 多次入境
S (single) 單次入境

12 **Issue Date** 簽證核發日

13 **Expiration Date** 簽證到期日

14 **Annotation** 註解

SCHENGEN
VISA
申根簽證

❶ **Valid For** 此證件適用於（申根國家）

❷ **From . . . Until . . .** 簽證有效期限

❸ **Type of Visa** 簽證種類

　　C (short term) 短期簽證

　　D (long term) 長期簽證

❹ **Number of Entries** 入境次數

　　mult 多次入境 / **single** 單次入境

❺ **Duration of Stay** 可停留時間

❻ **Issued In** 簽證辦理處

❼ **On (Date)** 簽證辦理時間

❽ **Number of Passport** 護照號碼

❾ **Surname, Name** 申辦人姓名

❿ **Remarks** 備註

2 機艙內
IN THE CABIN

DIALOGUE 1
Finding the Seat 找位子 010

A Where is my seat?

B Your seat number is 16A. Down this aisle, to your right.

A Thank you.

A Excuse me, but I think you're sitting in my seat.
What's your seat number?

C It's 17A. Oh, I'm sorry. I made a mistake.

A Don't worry about it.

A 請問我的位子在哪裡?

B 你的位子是16A，這邊的走道直走，在你右手邊的地方。

A 謝謝。

A 不好意思，你坐的這個位子好像是我的。請問你的位子是幾號?

C 是17A。哎，對不起，我弄錯了。

A 沒事的。

Study Points

down this aisle	沿著走道走	down作介系詞，是「沿著」的意思。
to your right	在你的右手邊	「to one's right」是「在你的右邊」，「to one's left」是「在你的左邊」。
Excuse me, but . . .	不好意思，……	but 後面接相反的意見，翻譯時不用把 but 翻出來。
I made a mistake.	我弄錯了。	用過去式表示為既成事實。
Don't worry about it.	請別在意。	更簡單的説法是：No problem. That's OK.

一般飛機上的座位都是從前面開始算起1、2、3……，從左邊算起是A、B、C……，登機時請再確定自己的座位號碼。

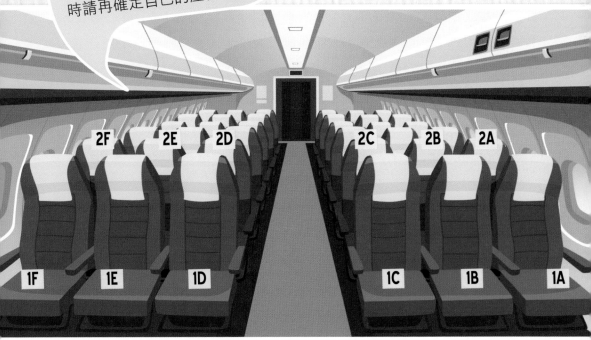

Having Lunch on the Plane 在機上用餐

Ⓐ What are my choices for lunch?

Ⓑ We have beef with rice and fish with noodles. Which would you like?

Ⓐ Fish with noodles, please.

Ⓑ Would you care for coffee or tea?

Ⓐ Coffee, please.

Ⓐ 午餐有什麼可以選？

Ⓑ 有牛肉飯和鮮魚麵，您要哪一種？

Ⓐ 我要鮮魚麵。

Ⓑ 要不要喝點咖啡或茶呢？

Ⓐ 請給我咖啡。

Study Points

What are my choices for . . . ?	我的⋯⋯選擇有什麼？	也可說「What do you have for . . . ?」（對於⋯⋯，你們有什麼？）。
Which would you like?	您想要哪一個？	使用 which 時，代表有提供對方選項。
Would you care for . . . ?	您想要⋯⋯嗎？／要不要來點⋯⋯？	「care for」表示喜歡、喜好。

ORDERING MEALS ON PLANES
機上點餐用語

F Flight attendant 空服員
P Passenger 乘客

F Would you like to have <u>fried rice</u> or <u>lasagna</u>?

您想要炒飯還是千層麵呢？

P I would like to have <u>lasagna</u>, please.
請給我千層麵。

F And what would you like to drink?
那您想要喝點什麼呢？

P What do you have here?
你們有什麼呢？

F We have <u>apple juice</u>, <u>orange juice</u>, and <u>oolong tea</u>.

我們有蘋果汁、柳橙汁和烏龍茶。

P I'll have <u>an orange juice</u>. Thank you.
請給我一杯柳橙汁，謝謝。

P Could you clean off my table, please?
你可以幫我清理一下桌面嗎？

F Sure.
當然可以。

1 captain 機長

2 flight attendant 空服員

3 passenger 旅客

4 carry-on baggage 登機行李

5 departure 出境

6 arrival 入境

7 check-in counter 報到櫃檯

8 terminal 航廈

9 waiting room 候機室

10 passport 護照

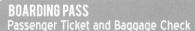 **boarding pass** 登機證

BOARDING PASS
Passenger Ticket and Baggage Check　First Class

GATE	BOARDING TIME	SEAT
6	14:30	3B

Class
First Class

Departure　　**Arrival**
Tokyo　　　　　New York

Ref No
046 15638 000621

BOARDING PASS
First Class

Gate:　6

Boarding
Time:　14:30

SEAT
3B

boarding gate 登機門

boarding time 登機時間

seat number 座號

Departures

Time	Destination	Flight	Gate	Status
12:00	Hong-Kong	HK4701	A56	Boarding
12:03	London	HT964	D15	Delayed
12:03	New York	HK4701	B56	Boarding
12:12	Amsterdam	HK487	C12	Cancelled
12:25	Buenos Aires	BA2578	B6	Boarding
12:26	Dusseldorf	DS4307	E4	Boarding
12:40	Oslo	OS258	B10	Boarding
12:55	Dubai	DB1234	C31	Boarding
13:03	Bologna	BL9875	A4	Boarding

departure time 起飛時間

overhead compartment 頭頂上方置物櫃

emergency exit 緊急出口

oxygen mask 氧氣罩

life jacket 救生衣

20 seat belt light 安全帶警示燈

21 reading light 閱讀燈

22 call button 呼叫鈕

23 blanket 毯子

24 pillow 枕頭

25 lavatory 廁所

26 vacant 空的

27 occupied 使用中

29 airsickness bag 嘔吐袋

28 airsick 暈機

FASTEN SEAT BELT WHILE SEATED
LIFE VEST UNDER YOUR SEAT
STOW CUP HOLDER DURING TAXI, TAKE - OFF AND LANDING

taxi 在這裡是
「（飛機）滑行」
的意思。

乘坐時請繫好安全帶
救生衣置於您的座位下方
飛機滑行、起飛和降落時，請闔上用餐板

help needed button 請求協助鈕　　fasten-seat-belt sign 安全帶指示燈

Useful Expressions

1 Excuse me. Can you show me where seat 23D is?
請問23D的座位在哪裡？

2 Excuse me. May I get through? 不好意思，借過一下。

3 Excuse me. Is this seat vacant? 不好意思，這位子有人坐嗎？

4 May I change seats with you? 我可以跟您換位子嗎？

5 Sorry, I think this is my seat. 不好意思，您坐到我的位子了。

6
Ⓐ Where can I put this bag?
Ⓑ Please put it in the overhead storage bin.
Ⓐ 這個行李可以放在哪裡？
Ⓑ 請放在上面的置物櫃。

7
Ⓐ Where can I leave my bag?
Ⓑ You can place your luggage under the seat in front of you.
Ⓐ 請問行李可以放在哪裡？
Ⓑ 您可以把行李放在前面的座位下方。

8 Can you please help me put my bag up there?
可以幫我把行李放上去嗎？

9 May I recline my seat? 我可以把椅背向後仰嗎？

2 機艙內的飲食

10
- Ⓐ What would you like to drink?
- Ⓑ What kind of drinks do you have?
- Ⓐ We have coffee, black tea, orange juice, tomato juice, beer, and wine.
- Ⓑ One tomato juice without ice, please.
- Ⓐ 請問您想喝什麼飲料？
- Ⓑ 有哪些飲料呢？
- Ⓐ 我們有咖啡、紅茶、柳橙汁、番茄汁、啤酒和葡萄酒。
- Ⓑ 請給我番茄汁，不加冰塊。

11 Would you like some coffee or tea? 請問您想要咖啡還是茶？

12 Some more coffee, please. 請再給我一些咖啡。

13
- Ⓐ Which would you like for dinner: beef, chicken, or fish?
- Ⓑ Fish, please.
- Ⓐ 請問您的晚餐想要吃牛肉、雞肉，還是魚肉？
- Ⓑ 我要魚肉，謝謝。

14 May I have a vegetarian meal instead? 請問可以換素食嗎？

15 Can you take my tray? 可以麻煩你把餐盤收走嗎？

16 I am a little hungry. Is there anything to eat?
我有點餓，請問有什麼可以吃的嗎？

17 Do you have any instant noodles? 你們有泡麵嗎？

AIRLINE MEAL
飛機上的餐飲

fried rice 炒飯

lasagna 千層麵

beef 牛肉

lamb 羊肉

pasta 義大利麵

fish 魚肉

SFML	Fish, Seafood	魚;海鮮
ORML	Oriental Meal	東方餐食（葷食）
AVML	Asian Vegetarian Meal	東方素食（無蛋奶、無蔥薑蒜）
VGML	Vegetarian Meal	西式素食（無奶、無蔥薑蒜）
BBML	Baby Meal	嬰兒餐
LSML	Low Sodium (Low-Salt Meal)	低鈉無鹽餐
HNML	Hindu Meal	印度教餐食（無牛肉）
MOML	Muslim Meal	伊斯蘭教餐食（無豬肉）
KSML	Kosher Meal	猶太教餐食（遵守猶太教之規定）

AIRLINE COMMON DRINKS
機上常見飲料

orange juice 柳橙汁

tomato juice 番茄汁

apple juice a 蘋果汁

cola 可樂

sprite 雪碧

diet cola 健怡可樂

orange soda 柳橙汽水

mineral water 礦泉水

oolong tea 烏龍茶

beer 啤酒

red wine 紅酒

white wine 白酒

whiskey 威士忌

gin and tonic 琴湯尼

Bloody Mary 血腥瑪麗

screwdriver 螺絲起子

vodka lime 伏特加萊姆

vodka rum 伏特加蘭姆

AIRLINE DISHES
機上餐

一般長程班機多半會印製菜單，放在座椅口袋內，或在飛機起飛後發給旅客，供旅客事先考慮想吃哪一種餐點。有些航空公司則是會在訂購機票時，詢問旅客是否要機上餐，到了機上便不再詢問乘客，而是直接依登記名冊發送餐點。

吃素的旅客，別忘了在訂機票或辦理登記時告訴航空公司人員，以便航空人員預先準備你的餐點。

18 May I please have a blanket and a pillow?
可以給我毛毯和枕頭嗎？

19 Do you have Chinese magazines or newspapers?
有中文雜誌或報紙嗎？

20 Do you sell tax-free goods on the flight?
機艙內有賣免稅商品嗎？

21 I'd like some water to take my medicine with.
我要吃藥，請給我一杯水。

22 Can I exchange my earphones? They don't work.
這副耳機沒有聲音，我可以換另外一副嗎？

23 How do I turn on the light? 請問要怎麼開燈？

24 I feel like vomiting. I need an airsickness bag.
我想吐，我需要嘔吐袋。

25 I feel sick. Can I have some medicine?
我覺得不舒服，有什麼藥可以給我服用嗎？

26 May I have some airsickness medicine? 請問有暈機藥嗎？

27 Would you mind checking on her?
可以請你看看她怎麼了嗎？

28 Is there a doctor on board? 飛機上有醫生嗎？

CAUTION SIGNS 飛機上的英文告示

Boeing 737-800 Safety Information

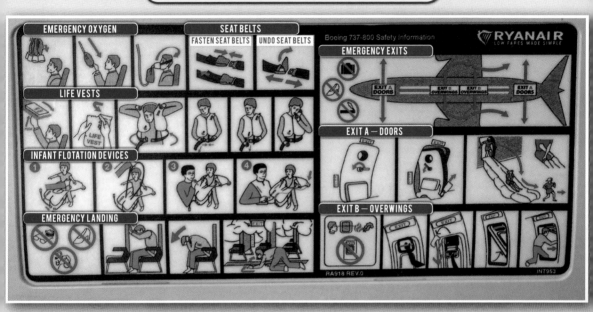

波音 737-800 安全設施使用方式

Emergency Oxygen 氧氣罩的使用

Seat Belts 安全帶的使用

   Fasten Seat Belts 繫上安全帶

   Undo Seat Belts 解開安全帶

Life Vests 救生衣的使用

Infant Flotation Devices 嬰兒漂浮設備

Emergency Landing 緊急降落措施

Emergency Exits 緊急逃生出口

Exit A–Doors 出口 A—機艙門

Exit B–Overwings 出口 B—翼上緊急出口

歡迎與介紹班機資訊

Ladies and gentlemen, welcome aboard Star Airlines flight 126 to Tokyo, Japan. Our flight time will be two hours and 45 minutes.

各位先生、女士您好,歡迎搭乘繁星航空第126次、飛往日本東京的班機,本次航行時間約為兩小時又45分鐘。

行李放置

Please secure all your baggage underneath the seat in front of you or in the overhead compartments.

請將您所有的行李放置於您前方的座椅底下,或置於頭頂上方的置物櫃。

繫安全帶與就定位置

Please fasten your seatbelt and stay in your seat. And please make sure your seat back is upright and your tray table is closed.

請繫妥安全帶、保持就坐,並確保您的椅背已豎直、餐桌已收起。

關閉電子設備

To ensure flight safety, please turn off all personal electronic devices such as cell phones and laptops.

為了確保飛航安全,請關閉您所有的電子產品,諸如手機與筆記型電腦。

Ladies and gentlemen, this is Flight Attendant Andrea Simpson speaking. On behalf of Air Garden Airlines, I would like to welcome you aboard Flight AG203 from San Francisco to Taipei. The flight time today is 10 hours and 30 minutes. Our expected time of arrival is 9:10 a.m. local time, July 7.

2
機艙內

AIRLINE ANNOUNCEMENTS
機上廣播

各位先生女士，我是空服員 Andrea Simpson，謹代表空中花園航空公司，歡迎各位搭乘從舊金山飛往台北的AG203班機。飛行時間預計是10小時30分鐘，我們預計會於台北當地時間7月7日上午9點10分抵達。

019

Good evening, passengers. This is your captain speaking. Welcome to Flight AG203, nonstop from San Francisco to Taipei. The weather ahead is good, and we should have a smooth flight. The time is 7:20 p.m. The cabin crew will be coming around in about twenty minutes to offer you a light snack and beverage. I'll talk to you again before we reach our destination. If you have any questions about our flight, please don't hesitate to ask one of our flight attendants. Relax and enjoy the flight. Thank you.

各位旅客，晚安，我是機長，歡迎搭乘從舊金山直飛台北的AG203班機。飛行天候良好，我們預計可以有一趟順利的飛行。現在時間是晚上7點20分，20分鐘之後，將會有空服員為您提供點心和飲料。在我們抵達目的地之前，我會再跟大家報告。如果您對此航班有任何問題，請儘管詢問我們的空服員。請放鬆好好享受這趟飛行，謝謝！

We are approaching an area of turbulence. For your safety and comfort, please go back to your seats and fasten your seat belts. Please keep your belts fastened until the "Seat Belt" sign goes off. Thank you.

本班機正接近亂流區，為了讓各位旅客能安全、舒適地度過，請各位旅客回到座位上，繫上安全帶，直到「繫上安全帶」的燈號熄滅為止，謝謝。

3 入境
IMMIGRATION

Immigration Inspection 入境審查

Ⓐ What's the purpose of your visit?

Ⓑ Sightseeing.

Ⓐ How long are you going to stay in the United States?

Ⓑ For seven days.

Ⓐ Where will you be staying?

Ⓑ I'll stay at the Hilton Hotel.

Ⓐ Do you have your return ticket?

Ⓑ Yes. Here it is.

Ⓐ 你來此的目的是什麼？

Ⓑ 觀光。

Ⓐ 你打算在美國停留多久？

Ⓑ 七天。

Ⓐ 你要住在哪裡？

Ⓑ 我住希爾頓大飯店。

Ⓐ 你有回程的機票嗎？

Ⓑ 有的，在這裡。

the purpose of your visit	此行目的	進入這個國家的目的
sightseeing	觀光	sightseer 則是指「觀光客」
Where will you be staying?	你會住在哪裡？	也可以説成： ① Where are you going to stay? ② Where will you stay?
return ticket	回程機票	來回機票是 round-trip ticket
Here it is.	東西在這裡。	把東西交給別人時，可以説： ① Here it is. ② Here you are.

Arrival

DIALOGUE 2
Baggage Inspection 行李檢查

A　Please bring your baggage here for inspection.

B　Here you are, officer.

A　Is all your baggage here?

B　Yes, a camera bag, a travel bag, and a suitcase.

A　Have you got anything to declare?

B　No. I have only personal effects.

A　請把您的行李拿過來這裡檢查。

B　好的，先生。

A　您所有的行李都在這裡了嗎？

B　是的，一個相機包、一個旅行袋和一個行李箱。

A　有什麼要申報的嗎？

B　沒有，我只有一些私人用品。

Study Points

inspection	檢驗；檢查	此為名詞，動詞為 inspect。
Is all your baggage here?	你所有的行李都在這裡了嗎？	baggage 為不可數名詞，要用 is。
declare	申報	此為動詞，名詞為 declaration。
personal effects	私人物品	effect 作複數使用時，意指「財物；財產」。

CUSTOMS DECLARATION
海關申報

如果有東西需要申報，須至「申報」（declare）的櫃檯；若不需申報，則至「不申報」（nothing to declare）的櫃檯。這時須出示海關申報表與護照，有時須打開行李供海關人員檢查。

1 **arrival time** 到站時間

2 **arrival terminal** 到站航廈

3 **arrival hall** 入境大廳

4 **baggage hall** 行李提取大廳

5 **baggage claim** 行李提領

6 **lost and found** 遺失行李詢問處

7 **passport control** 護照檢查

8 **immigration** 入境審查

9 **immigration form; disembarkation card** 入境申請表

10 immigration inspection
入境檢查

11 customs 海關

12 customs control 海關管制

13 customs inspection 海關檢驗

14 customs declaration form
海關申報表

15 customs duties 關稅

16 declare 申報

17 cash 現金

18 tax-free articles
免稅品

19 prohibited articles
違禁品

20 cigarette 菸

21 liquor 酒類飲料

22 time difference 時差

23 jet lag 時差失調

ARRIVAL
入境程序

入境時需要準備的文件包括：

1. 護照
2. 海關申報書
3. 外籍人士另需 (1) 簽證 (2) 機票 (3) 入境登記表

Step 1

Disembarkation

下飛機

Step 3

Baggage claim

提領行李

辦完入境手續後，就可以到行李提領處
領取自己的行李。如果找不到行李，
可以向工作人員出示**行李標籤（claim
tag）**，請他們幫忙尋找。

Step 2

Immigration inspection

入境審查

準備好護照和**入境申請表**
（disembarkation card），有時也會
被要求附上回程機票。審查人員可能會
詢問你的入境目的、居留時間、住宿地
點、持有多少現金等問題。

Step 4

Customs inspection

海關檢查

須出示護照及關稅申報表，海關人員會問是
否需要申報物品，有時會要求打開行李接受
檢查。在接受入境檢查或海關檢查時，回答
應該具體且明確。

Step 5

Baggage inspection

檢查行李

I-94 表格
I-94 Form

I-94表格為出入美國時所需填寫的入境表格，現已數位化。旅客在入境美國時，只需注意更新自己的EVUS（Electronic Visa Update System 簽證更新電子系統），並在機上填寫右頁的海關申報表即可。

DEPARTMENT OF HOMELAND SECURITY
U.S. Customs and Border Protection

OMB No. 1651-0111

Admission Number

Welcome to the United States

392923282 18

I-94 Arrival/Departure Record - Instructions

1. This form must be completed by all persons except U.S. Citizens, returning resident aliens, aliens with immigrant visas, and Canadian Citizens visiting or in transit.

2. Type or print legibly with pen in ALL CAPITAL LETTERS. Use English. Do not write on the back of this form.

3. This form is in two parts. Please complete both the Arrival Record (Items 1 through 13) and the Departure Record (Items 14 through 17).

4. When all items are completed, present this form to the CBP Officer.

5. Item 7 - If you are entering the United States by land, enter **LAND** in this space. If you are entering the United States by ship, enter **SEA** in this space.

CBP Form I-94 (10/04)

Admission Number

OMB No. 1651-0111

392923282 18

Arrival Record

6. Family Name

7. First (Given) Name

8. Birth Date (Day/Mo/Yr) — 9. / 10. / 11.

12. Country of Citizenship

13. Sex (Male or Female) — 14.

15. Passport Number

16. Airline and Flight Number

17. Country Where You Live — 18. City Where You Boarded

19. City Where Visa was Issued — 20. Date Issued (Day/Mo/Yr)

21. Address While in the United States (Number and Street)

22. City and State

CBP Form I-94 (10/04)

Departure Number

OMB No. 1651-0111

392923282 18

I-94 Departure Record

14. Family Name

15. First (Given) Name — 16. Birth Date (Day/Mo/Yr)

17. Country of Citizenship

CBP Form I-94 (10/04)

See Other Side

STAPLE HERE

1. This form must be completed by all persons except U.S. citizens, returning resident aliens, aliens with immigrant visas, and Canadian Citizens visiting or in transit. 所有人都必須填寫此表格，除了美國公民、返回美國的永久居民外籍人士、持移民簽證首次入境的新移民外籍人士、入境美國的加拿大公民或是過境的外籍旅客。

2. Type or print legibly with pen in ALL CAPITAL LETTERS. Use English. Do not write on the back of this form. 請用大寫字母打字或用筆填寫清楚，使用英文填寫，不要在此表背面寫任何字。

3. This form is in two parts. Please complete both the Arrival Record (Item 1 through 13) and the Departure Record (Item 14 through 17). 此表包括兩部分，請填寫入境記錄（第1項至第13項）和離境記錄（第14項至第17項）兩部分。

4. When all items are completed, present this form to the U.S. Immigration and Naturalization Service Inspector. 填寫完畢後，請將此表交給美國移民局官員。

5. Item 7—If you are entering the United States by land, enter LAND in this space. If you are entering the United States by ship, enter SEA in this space. 第 7 項內容說明──如果您是從陸路進入美國，請在空格內填寫LAND。如果您是搭乘船隻進入美國，請在空格內填寫 SEA。

6. Family Name 姓氏

7. First (Given) Name 名字

8. Birth Date 生日

9. Day (D) 日

10. Mo (M) 月

11. Yr (Y) 年

12. Country of Citizenship 國籍

13. Sex 性別

14. Male (M) / Female (F) 男性／女性

15. Passport Number 護照號碼

16. Airline and Flight Number 航空公司與航班號碼

17. Country Where You Live 居住國家

18. City Where You Boarded 登機／登船城市

19. City Where Visa Was Issued 簽證核發城市

20. Date Issued 簽證核發時間

21. Address While in the United States (Number and Street) 在美國期間的居住地點（街道與號碼）

22. City and State 城市與州名

海關申報表
Customs Declaration Form

U.S. Customs and
Border Protection

Customs Declaration

① Each arriving traveler or responsible family member must provide the following information (only ONE written declaration per family is required)

1. Family Name ②

③ First (Given)　　　　　　　　　　　Middle

④ 2. Birth date　Day ⑤　Month ⑥　Year ⑦

⑧ 3. Number of Family members traveling with you

⑨ 4. (a) U.S. Street Address (hotel name/destination)

　　(b) City ⑩　　　　　　　(c) State ⑪

⑫ 5. Passport Issued by (country)

⑬ 6. Passport number

⑭ 7. Country of Residence

⑮ 8. Countries visited on this trip prior to U.S. arrival

⑯ 9. Airline/Flight Number or Vessel Name

⑰ 10. The primary purpose of this trip is business.　Yes　No

⑱ 11. I am (We are) bringing

　(a) fruits, vegetables, plants, food, insects　Yes　No

　(b) meats, animals, animal/wildlife products　Yes　No

　(c) disease agents, cell cultures, or snails　Yes　No

　(d) soil or have you visited a farm/ranch/pasture　Yes　No

⑲ 12. I have (We have) been in close proximity of (such as touching or handling) livestock　Yes　No

⑳ 13. I am (We are) carrying currency or monetary instrument over $10,000 U.S. or foreign equivalent (see definition of monetary instrument on reverse)　Yes　No

㉑ 14. I have (We have) commercial merchandise? (articles for sale, samples used for soliciting orders, or goods that are not considered personal effects.)　Yes　No

㉒ 15. Residents — the total value of all goods, including commercial merchandise I/we have purchased or acquired abroad. (including gifts for someone else, but not items mailed to the U.S.) and am/are bringing to the U.S. is　$

㉓ Visitors — the total value of all articles that will remain in the U.S. including commercial merchandise is:　$

Read the instruction on the back of this form. Space is provided to list all the items you might declare.

I HAVE READ THE IMPORTANT INFORMATION ON THE REVERSE SIDE OF THIS FORM AND HAVE MADE A TRUTHFUL DECLARATION.

㉔ X _____

(Signature)　　　　　　　　　Date (day/month/year)

For Official Use Only

CBP Form 00540 (0104)

---

① Each arriving traveler or responsible family member must provide the following information (only ONE written declaration per family is required) 每位入境旅客或家庭代表均須填妥下列資料（每個家庭只需填寫一張）

② Family Name 姓

③ First (Given) Name 名

④ Birth Date 生日

⑤ Day 日

⑥ Month 月

⑦ Year 年

⑧ Number of Family members traveling with you 同行家屬人數（不包含自己）

⑨ U.S. Street Address (hotel name/destination) 美國居住地址（飯店／目的地名稱）

⑩ City 城市名

⑪ State 州名

⑫ Passport Issued by (country) 護照發照國家

⑬ Passport number 護照號碼

⑭ Country of Residence 居住國家

⑮ Countries visited on this trip prior to U.S. arrival 此趟行程抵美前，還去哪些國家

⑯ Airline/Flight Number or Vessel Name 航空公司／班機號碼或船艦名稱

⑰ The primary purpose of this trip is business. 此行主要目的為洽公

⑱ I am (We are) bringing 我攜帶了

(a) fruits, vegetables, plants, food, insects 蔬果、植物、食物、昆蟲

(b) meats, animals, animal/wildlife products 肉品、動物、動物製品

(c) disease agents, cell cultures, or snails 病原體、細胞培養、蝸牛

(d) soil or have you visited a farm/ranch/pasture 土壤，或您曾造訪農場

⑲ I have (We have) been in close proximity of (such as touching or handling) livestock 我（我們）曾經近距離接觸家畜

⑳ I am (We are) carrying currency or monetary instrument over $10,000 U.S. or foreign equivalent 我（我們）攜帶了超過一萬美元或等值貨幣

㉑ I have (We have) commercial merchandise? (articles for sale, samples used for soliciting orders, or goods that are not considered personal effects.) 我（我們）有攜帶商品？（販賣之商品、訂購之樣本等任何非屬私人之物品）

㉒ Residents（美國居民才須填寫）

㉓ Visitors — the total value of all articles that will remain in the U.S. including commercial merchandise（遊客填寫）攜帶商品總值

㉔ 填妥表格後，在此處簽名

Useful Expressions

❶
- Ⓐ May I see your passport, please?
- Ⓑ ① Here it is.
  - ② Here you are.
- Ⓐ 請出示護照。
- Ⓑ 好的，在這裡。

❷ What is the purpose of your visit? 你此行目的是什麼？

❸
- ① Just sightseeing.
- ② I've come for sightseeing.
- ③ I'm here as a tourist. 觀光。

❹
- ① On business.
- ② I'm here on business. 出差。

❺ Half for business and half for pleasure.
一半是為了工作，一半是旅遊。

❻
- ① I'm here as a foreign student.
- ② I'm here to attend a university. 我是來留學的。

❼ I've come to study at a language school.
我是來語言學校唸書的。

❽ To visit a friend. 來拜訪朋友的。

9

A　① How long are you going to stay?
　　② How long do you plan to stay?

B　① I'll be here for three weeks.
　　② About two weeks.
　　③ A couple of months.

A　你打算停留多久呢？

B　① 三個星期。
　　② 大約兩個星期。
　　③ 兩、三個月。

10

A
1. Where are you going to stay?
2. Where will you stay?

B
1. At the Hilton Hotel downtown.
2. I'll stay with a friend in New York.
3. I'll be staying with my younger sister's family.
4. I'll be staying at my friend's home.

A 你打算住在哪裡？

B
1. 我打算住在市中心的希爾頓大飯店。
2. 我會住在我紐約朋友的家中。
3. 我會住在我妹妹那裡。
4. 我會去住我朋友家。

11

A How much money do you have?

B About $1,000.

A 你帶了多少現金？

B 大約1,000塊美金。

12 Do you have your return ticket? 你有回程機票嗎？

13

A May I see your return ticket?

B
1. Here it is.
2. This is my return ticket.

A 麻煩給我看你的回程機票。

B
1. 好的，在這裡。
2. 這是我的回程機票。

2 提領行李 ⌈025⌉

14
- Ⓐ Where is the baggage claim area for Flight 212?
- Ⓑ It's number 7.
- Ⓐ 請問212號班機的行李在哪裡提領？
- Ⓑ 在7號。

15 I can't find my luggage. 我找不到我的行李。

16 My luggage is missing. 我的行李不見了。

17 Here is my claim tag. 這是我的行李標籤。

18
- Ⓐ What kind of bag is it?
- Ⓑ ① It's a green suitcase.
  - ② It's about this size.
  - ③ It's a medium-sized suitcase with my name tag on it.
- Ⓐ 是什麼樣的行李？
- Ⓑ ① 是個綠色的手提箱。
  - ② 大概是這個尺寸的大小。
  - ③ 是中型的手提箱，行李牌上有我的名字。

19 How soon will you deliver my luggage?
我的行李大概什麼時候會到？

20 Please deliver my luggage to the Hilton Hotel.
麻煩你把行李送到希爾頓大飯店。

21 My suitcase is badly damaged. 我的手提箱嚴重受損了。

22

   A Do you have anything to declare?

   B ① No, I have nothing to declare.
      ② I have something to declare.
      ③ Just this.

   A 你有什麼要申報的物品嗎？

   B ① 我沒有要申報的物品。
      ② 我有要申報的物品。
      ③ 只有這個要申報。

23

   A What is their approximate value?

   B About $120.00.

   A 這些物品的價值大約是多少？

   B 大約是120塊美金。

24 You'll have to pay duty on this. Please declare this at the window over there.
這個物品是要課稅的，請到那邊那個窗口去申報。

25 It's a souvenir for my friend. 這是要給朋友的紀念品。

26 It's for my personal use. 這是我的私人用品。

27

   A Do you have any liquor or cigarettes?

   B I have two bottles of whiskey.

   A 你有攜帶酒或香菸嗎？

   B 我有帶兩瓶威士忌。

28

(A) Do you have any fruit or vegetables?

(B) I have this box of fruit. It's a gift.

(A) 你有攜帶水果或蔬菜嗎？

(B) 我有帶一箱水果，是送人的禮物。

29 I'm sorry. You're not allowed to bring in fruit.

很抱歉，水果是禁止攜帶入境的。

30 OK. You can pass through.

好了，沒問題，你可以通行了。

台灣出入境須知

❶ 入境可以帶幾條菸？幾瓶酒？超過數量時要如何處理？

旅客須滿20歲以上，入境時每人限帶捲菸200支，或雪茄25支，或菸絲1磅。
酒1公升為限，超過的數量應主動向關稅局或海關申請辦理課稅，以免受罰。

❷ 我可以帶多少台幣及美金入出境？

1. **新台幣**：新台幣100,000元為限，如超過限額，應在入境或出境前事先向中央
   銀行申請核准；超額部分未經核准，不准攜入或攜出，若未申報，超過新台
   幣10萬元部分沒收；申報不實者，超過申報部分沒收。

2. **外幣**：攜帶外幣入境不予限制，但超過等值美金10,000元現金者，應報明海關
   登記，未經申報依法沒入。

3. **人民幣**：人民幣20,000元為限。如超過限額，應自動向海關申報，並自行封存
   於海關，出境時准予攜出；如申報不實，超過部分，依法沒入。

4. **有價證券**：總面額逾等值10,000美元者，應向海關申報。未依規定申報或申報
   不實者，科以相當於未申報或申報不實之有價證券價額之罰鍰。

5. **黃金**：不予限制，但應於入、出境時向海關申報，如總額超過美金20,000元，
   應向經濟部國際貿易局申請輸入許可證，並辦理報關驗放手續。

❸ 我可以攜帶肉製品入境嗎？

為了防範豬瘟進入台灣，2018/12/18起，私自挾帶豬肉製品，初犯罰20萬、累犯
100萬。肉乾、香腸、臘肉、火腿、肉製零食、真空包裝等非罐頭食品，現在均
不得攜帶入境。

5 租借 Wi-Fi 分享器 🎧027

31

A I'd like to rent a portable Wi-Fi router for five days.
我想要租借攜帶型Wi-Fi分享器五天。

B How do I return the router at the end of my trip?
在我旅途結束後，要怎麼歸還分享器？

32

A What's the ID and password for this router?
這台分享器的帳號和密碼是什麼？

B The ID and password are on the back of the router.
帳號和密碼就在分享器背面。

33 Included with your router are a USB cable and an AC adaptor.
除了分享器之外，還有附帶一條USB線和電源轉接器。

USB cable
USB 線

AC adaptor
電源轉接器

Wi-Fi router
Wi-Fi 分享器

SIM card
(subscriber identification card)
SIM 卡

美國入境須知

美國政府為防範恐怖分子，從 2004 年 10 月 26 日起，實施 US-VISIT 安檢系統，要求入境之外國旅客於入關時掃描十指的指紋，以查驗身分。美國移民官員如果懷疑入境者之身分、證件或來美之目的，可以拒絕旅客入境，並予以遣返。

入境美國應誠實申報隨身所攜帶之財物，不可攜帶違禁物品，如申報不實或未申報，物品有可能被沒收，或遭受民、刑事處分。

以下是一些相關規定：

01 個人隨身攜帶入境物品（含商品及禮品）之免稅額，美國居民為 800 美元，非美國居民為 100 美元；酒類免稅額為一公升（攜帶者須年滿 21 歲）；菸類免稅額為一條菸，或五十枝雪茄，或二公斤菸草。古巴出產之雪茄及香菸禁止攜入。

02 禮物不應包裝，以便海關檢查。

03 可攜帶之現金及證券額度為一萬美元。超過額度者，須事先向海關申報，倘若未先行申報而經查獲者，將遭受民、刑事懲罰，現金及證券亦將被沒收。

04 旅客不得攜帶管制農（畜）產品及動物入境美國，倘若未申報而經查獲者，除該產品將被沒收外，並可能被處以罰金。

1 May I see your passport, please? 請出示護照好嗎？

- **Here you are.** 來。（遞出護照）
- **Here is my passport.** 這是我的護照。
- **Sure. Here are my passport and declaration form.**
  當然，這是我的護照和關稅申報表。

2 What is the purpose of your stay/visit? 您此行的目的是什麼？

- **I'm here on __vacation__ .** (tour/vacation/business)
  我是來度假的。
- **Sightseeing.** 觀光。
- **I'm visiting a friend.** 我是來探望朋友的。

3 What is your final destination? 您的目的地是哪裡？

- **I'm going to __New York__ .** 我要去紐約。
- **I'm here to transfer to __London__ .** 我是來這要轉機去倫敦的。

4 How long are you going to stay? 您會在這待多久？

- **I will stay here for __3__ days.** 我會在這待三天。

5 Where will you stay? 您會住在哪裡？

- **I'm staying at hotels.** 我會住在飯店。
- **I will stay at a friend's place.** 我會住在朋友家。

6 How much money are you carrying? 您身上攜帶了多少現金？

- **I have __$10,000__ .** 我身上有一萬美金。

個人相關問題
Personal Questions

1 Where are you from?　您來自哪裡？
- I'm from Taiwan.　我來自台灣。

2 What do you do? / What's your occupation?　您的職業是？
- I'm a __teacher__ .　我是一名教師。

3 Have you ever been here before?　您之前有來過這裡嗎？
- Yes, I've been here _5_ times.　有的，我來過這裡 5 次。
- No. This is my first time here.　沒有，這是我第一次來。

4 Are you traveling alone?　您是一個人來的嗎？
- Yes, I'm traveling here alone.　是的，我一個人來。
- No, I'm with my family/friend.　不，我跟我家人／朋友一起。

5 Do you have any relatives or friends here?
您在本地有親戚或朋友嗎？
- Yes. My ___aunt___ is living here.　有的，我的阿姨住在這裡。
- No, I don't know anyone here.　不，我在這裡沒有認識的人。

passport control 護照查驗處

At the immigration counter 入境櫃檯

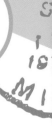

4 兌換錢幣
CHANGING CURRENCY

Can you Change This Into Dollars? 請把這個換成美金

Ⓐ Can you change this into dollars?

Ⓑ How would you like it?

Ⓐ I'd like ten twenties, five tens, and the rest in change.

Ⓑ Certainly, sir.

Ⓐ By the way, how much is the commission?

Ⓑ One percent.

Ⓐ 請把這個換成美金。

Ⓑ 請問要換哪些種類的面額？

Ⓐ 我要20塊美金的10張、10塊美金的5張，剩下的請換成零錢。

Ⓑ 好的，先生。

Ⓐ 對了，手續費是多少？

Ⓑ 1%。

Study Points

change . . . into . . .	將…… 兌換成……	也可以説： • change . . . to . . . • change . . . for . . .
How would you like it?	要換哪幾種面額？	兌換外幣時，常會被問到這個問題。
ten twenties, five tens	20 塊的 10 張、10 塊的 5 張	紙鈔是 bill，銅板是 coin。
How much is the commission?	手續費是多少錢？	commission 是「佣金」。

一般在機場、車站的銀行兌換處，或是市區銀行、飯店等地方，都可以兌換外幣，但是以下有幾點要特別注意的地方是：

1. 機場、車站和飯店的匯率都比市區銀行要來得高，所以在這些地方最好只要兌換小金額就好，如果兌換的金額大的話，到市區的銀行兌換較為划算。

2. 因為每次兌換錢幣都會收取手續費，所以最好減少兌換的次數。

3. 因為零錢無法再兌換，因此最好能全部用完。

4. 兌換剩餘的當地貨幣時，需要出示兌換證明書，所以要保管好。

5. 兌換旅行支票時會用到護照，所以要先準備好。

I'd Like to Change US Dollars Into Euros.
我想把美金換成歐元。

A   I'd like to change some US dollars into euros and I'd like to know today's exchange rate.

B   According to today's exchange rate, every US dollar in cash is equivalent to 0.75 euros.

A   Is there any service charge?

B   We charge a €1 commission on each deal. How much would you like to change?

A   400 US dollars. Here it is. Would you please give me small bills?

B   No problem.

A   我想把這些美金換成歐元，請問今天的匯率是多少？

B   根據外匯牌價，今天是一美元兌換0.75歐元。

A   要付手續費嗎？

B   每筆交易的手續費是一歐元。您想換多少？

A   四百美元，給妳。麻煩換小鈔給我好嗎？

B   好的。

Study Points

exchange rate	匯率	exchange 為「交換」之意。
is equivalent to	等同於……	「等同於……」的用法為「be equivalent to」。
service charge	手續費	charge 為「索費；收費」。
small bills	小鈔（面額較小的鈔票）	大鈔為「large bills」。

在國外的領錢方式 & 注意事項：
How to Withdraw Money in a Foreign Country

1 提款卡（**ATM card**）

許多銀行或是郵局的提款卡，都需要事前申辦國外交易功能，才可在國外領錢；且會有跨國提款密碼，才能提領當地貨幣。（每家銀行的提領手續費與每日每筆限額不同）

2 信用卡（**credit card**）

若是使用信用卡在海外提款，等同於預借現金，依每家銀行可能會有不同的借貸利率與手續費，此部分宜先查明再行提領。

3 簽帳金融卡（**debit card**）

連結了個人銀行帳戶的金融卡，可提款也可消費。消費前需先匯款至帳戶才可進行刷卡，消費時則直接從帳戶扣除，有多少扣多少，不會產生超刷、透支或產生循環利息的款項。用簽帳金融卡在國外消費也依各家銀行而有不同的手續費金額產生。

1 currency exchange counter 貨幣兌換處

2 currency 通貨；流通貨幣

3 foreign currency 外幣

5 bill 紙幣

6 coin 硬幣；錢幣

4 cash 現金

7 small change 零錢

8 check 支票

10 **signature** 簽名

9 **traveler's check**
旅行支票

11 **exchange rate** 匯率

12 **exchange receipt** 兌換證明

13 **commission** 手續費

14 **ID card** 身分證

15 **bankbook** 存摺

16 **account** 戶頭

17 **savings account** 儲蓄帳戶

18 **deposit account** 存款帳戶

19 **checking account** 支票帳戶

1 兌幣時的用語 033

❶ Where can I change money? 兌換處在哪裡？

❷ Where is the nearest bank? 最近的銀行在哪裡？

❸ I'd like to change NT dollars into US dollars.
我想把台幣兌換成美金。

❹ Can you change American dollars into British pounds?
可以幫我把美金換成英鎊嗎？

❺ Can you break this into small change?
可以幫我把這些錢換成零錢嗎？

❻ Can you break this $100 bill?
可以幫我把這100塊美金換成零錢嗎？

❼ Please include some small change. 請同時換些零錢。

❽ Five tens, ten fives, and the rest in quarters, please.
請給我5張10塊美金、10張5塊美金，其餘的換成25分錢的硬幣。

❾ I'd like it all in twenties, please. 請全部換成20塊美金。

❿ Can you please cash this check and give me ten twenty-dollar bills and twenty five-dollar bills?
請將這張支票換成10張20塊的美金，以及20張5塊的美金。

歐美國家
使用硬幣

美元硬幣

dollar ($) 美金
1 dollar 美金一元
half dollar = 50 cents 美金五十分
quarter = 25 cents 美金二十五分
dime = 10 cents 美金十分
nickel = 5 cents 美金五分
penny = 1 cent 美金一分

英鎊硬幣

pound sterling (£) 英鎊
1 pound 一英鎊
penny 便士
（複數為 pence）
（1 pound = 100 pence）

歐元硬幣

euro (€) 歐元
1 euro 一歐元
euro cent 歐分
（1 euro = 100 euro cents）

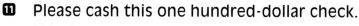

⓫ Please cash this one hundred-dollar check.
請把這張100塊美金的支票換成現金。

⓬ Can you break it down like this?
（將紙條拿給對方看）請照這張紙上所寫的方式換錢。

⓭ What's the exchange rate for euros?
歐元的兌換匯率是多少？

⓮ What commission do you charge? 手續費是多少錢？

15 Can I have an exchange receipt? 可以給我交易收據嗎？

16 The amount of money is not right. 這金額錯了。

ATM
(= automatic teller machine)
自動提款機

Cash machine

2 匯款或開戶的用語

17 I'd like to get a remittance from Taiwan.
我想領台灣寄來的匯款。

18 How can I get a remittance from Taiwan?
我要怎麼領取台灣寄來的匯款？

19 I'd like to transfer some money. 我想要匯款。

20 I'd like to open an account. 我想要開戶。

21 Will you tell me how to open a savings account?
你可以教我怎麼開戶嗎？

22 Ⓐ What kind of account would you like to open?
     Ⓑ A savings account, please.
     Ⓐ 您要開哪種戶頭呢？
     Ⓑ 我要開活期存款的戶頭。

23 I'd like to make a deposit. 我想要存款。

24 I'd like to withdraw $400 from my account.
我想從戶頭提出400塊美金。

BANK VOCABULARY
銀行常用動詞

1	**open** an account	開戶頭
2	**close** an account	結清戶頭
3	**deposit** money	存錢
4	**make** a deposit	存錢
5	**withdraw** money	提錢
6	**cash** a check	兌現支票
7	**apply** for a loan	申請貸款
8	**borrow** money	借錢
9	**lend** money	放款
10	**purchase**	買進
11	**speak** to the manager	找經理談
12	**check** my account balance	查戶頭餘額
13	**transfer** money	轉帳

5 飯店
HOTELS

DIALOGUE 1
Checking In 辦理入住手續 (035)

- Ⓐ I'd like to check in, please. The name is Louis Lee. I made a reservation from Taiwan.

- Ⓑ Just a moment, please. Yes, Mr. Louis Lee, a single room for three nights. Is that right?

- Ⓐ Yes, that's right.

- Ⓑ Would you like to pay in cash or with a credit card?

- Ⓐ Cash, please.

- Ⓑ Will you fill out this form, please?

- Ⓐ 我要辦住房手續。訂房名字是路易斯‧李，我是在台灣訂房的。
- Ⓑ 請稍等。路易斯‧李先生，您是訂三個晚上的單人房，是嗎？
- Ⓐ 是的，沒錯。
- Ⓑ 您要用現金付款，還是用信用卡付？
- Ⓐ 我要用現金。
- Ⓑ 可以幫我填寫這張表格嗎？

Study Points

I'd like to check in, please.	我要辦住房手續。	check in 的名詞是 check-in；退房則是 check out
made a reservation	已預約	reservation 的動詞是 reserve
a single room for three nights	三個晚上的單人房	single room 也可以說成 single
pay in cash or with a credit card	付現還是刷卡	刷卡也可以說「pay by credit card」
fill out this form	填寫這個表格	fill out 指「填寫」（表格等）

Hotel

在飯店辦理住宿手續的慣用說法是：

- **I'd like to check in, please.**
- **Check in, please.**

然後再告訴對方自己的名字，以及有事先訂房：

My name is . . . I have a reservation.

這時櫃檯會從訂房名單中找出你的名字，並且給你一份住宿單，請你登記一些基本資料。寫的時候最好能確定房間的種類（single、double、twin）、費用及住宿的天數等，最後再領住房卡就行了。

DIALOGUE 2

Checking In With an Online Reservation
以網路預約辦理住宿登記

Ⓐ Good afternoon, sir. Are you checking in?

Ⓑ Yes. I've booked a single room for two nights.

Ⓐ May I ask how you made the reservation?

Ⓑ I did it online through a hotel-booking service.

Ⓐ OK. I'll need your last name and your booking confirmation code.

Ⓑ My last name is Peters, and the confirmation code is CY4587GB.

Ⓐ Thank you, Mr. Peters.
[searches for the booking]
Yes, your room is ready for you now.

Ⓐ 先生，午安。請問您要辦理住宿登記嗎？

Ⓑ 是的，我有預訂兩晚的單人房。

Ⓐ 請問您是透過哪裡預訂的呢？

Ⓑ 我是在一個訂飯店的網站線上預訂的。

Ⓐ 好的，請告訴我您的姓氏以及訂房確認代碼。

Ⓑ 我姓彼得斯，我的確認代碼是 CY4587GB。

Ⓐ 謝謝您，彼得斯先生。
〔尋找預訂資訊〕
有了，您的房間已經準備好了。

Study Points

for two nights	兩晚	訂了幾晚，介系詞用 for。
through a hotel-booking service	透過飯店網站	「透過……」的介系詞為 through。
last name	姓氏	姓氏也可稱作 surname；名字為 first name。
confirmation code	確認代碼	confirmation 為名詞，動詞為 confirm。

現在透過網路訂房非常便利，線上預訂飯店的網站也越來越多，除了可自行比較房型、也可查看網友住宿後的評價。在出發前，也能事先跟飯店方聯繫，約定入住時間與特殊要求。

當我們進入到飯店的房間，整個人一下子就會鬆懈下來。有人可能感覺像回到家一樣，不知不覺中製造出意想不到的麻煩。以下舉出幾點在歐美的飯店中應注意的事項。

1 要給幫我們提行李的 bellboy（旅館的侍者）或 porter（大飯店搬運行李的服務生）小費。通常一件行李是給一塊美金，給小費的時候記得要跟對方說聲謝謝。

2 即使人待在房間裡也要鎖門。如果有人敲門，不要將房門全部打開，應先問對方是誰：「Who is it?」等確定好是誰之後再開。有些人就是因為沒有弄清楚就隨便開門而遭到搶劫。

3 最常發生的問題，就是把鑰匙放在房間裡，忘記帶出來。因為飯店房間的門幾乎都是屬於自動上鎖的，因此只要離開房間就一定要記得帶鑰匙。萬一真的被關在門外，只好去跟櫃檯的人員說：「I'm locked out.」請他們來幫你開門。

4 就算房門上了鎖，也不見得絕對保險。像現金或是平時不需要用到的護照等貴重物品，除了放在保險箱，也可以詢問櫃檯人員是否幫忙保管：「Will you keep my valuables?」

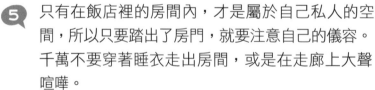

5 只有在飯店裡的房間內，才是屬於自己私人的空間，所以只要踏出了房門，就要注意自己的儀容。千萬不要穿著睡衣走出房間，或是在走廊上大聲喧嘩。

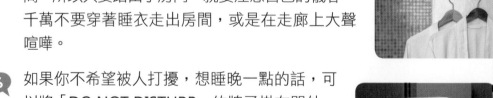

6 如果你不希望被人打擾，想睡晚一點的話，可以將「DO NOT DISTURB」的牌子掛在門外。如果外出時希望有人來清掃房間，則可以掛上「PLEASE MAKE UP THE ROOM」的牌子。

1 Front Office 客務部

Reservation 訂房
Reception 櫃檯接待
Operator 總機
Cashier 出納（屬財務部 Financing）
Business Center 商務中心
Service Center; Concierge 服務中心
・Doorman 門房
・Bellhop 行李員
・Driver 駕駛
・Flight Greeter 機場接待

2 Housekeeping 房務部

Housekeeping 房務組
（又稱 Room Maid 房務人員）
Cleaning 清潔組（負責公共區域）
Laundry Room 洗衣房
Linen Room 布巾室（房務部的心臟地帶）
Lost and Found 遺失物品管理
Florist 花房
Butler 客房值勤服務員（管家服務）

3 F & B (Food & Beverage Department) 餐飲部

Dining 餐廳部
Kitchen 廚房
Steward 餐務部（餐具管理、廢棄物管理）
Room Service 客房餐飲

Front of the House
前場
房客可接觸的區域

Security 安全室（門禁管制、停車場管理）
Engineering 工程部
Purchasing 採購部
Sales & Marketing 行銷業務部
Financing 財務部
Human Resources 人力資源部
Public Relations 公關部
Information 資訊部

Back of the House
後場
房客不可進入的區域

1 hotel 飯店；旅館

2 motel 汽車旅館

3 villa 渡假村旅館

4 youth hostel 青年旅館

5 bed & breakfast 民宿　　**6 spa** 水療飯店

7 lobby 大廳

8 front desk;
reception desk 櫃檯

9 doorman 門房

10 receptionist 櫃檯人員

11 operator 總機人員

12 bellhop; porter 行李員

13 room attendant 客房服務員

14 reservation 訂房

15 check in 辦理住房

16 check out 辦理退房

17 housephone 內線電話

18 morning call; wake-up call 晨喚服務

19 room (meal) service 客房餐飲服務

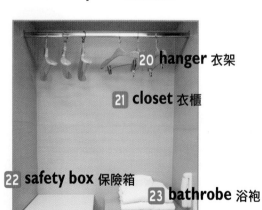

20 hanger 衣架

21 closet 衣櫃

22 safety box 保險箱

23 bathrobe 浴袍

24 refrigerator 冰箱

hotel charges 住宿費
extra charge 額外費用
bill 帳單
receipt 收據
amount 金額
service charge 服務費
dining charge 餐費

single room 單人房

twin room 雙床房

double room 雙人房

＊在美國，double room
有時也指 twin room

triple room 三人房

suite 套房

presidential suite 總統套房

1 飯店預約

❶ I'd like to reserve a hotel room for tonight.
我想訂今晚的客房。

❷ Do you have a room available for tomorrow night?
你們明天晚上有空房嗎？

❸ Is there a room available for Wednesday and Thursday nights? 星期三和星期四晚上有空房嗎？

❹ I'd like to stay for three nights. 我想住三個晚上。

❺ Do you have a twin room? 你們有空的雙床房間嗎？

❻ What kind of room do you have in mind?
您想住什麼樣的房間？

❼ I'd like a double room. 我要一間雙人房。

❽ I'd like a single room with a bath.
我要一間含衛浴設備的單人房。

❾ How much is it per night? 住宿一晚要多少錢？

❿ How much is a single room? 單人房是多少錢？

⓫ Is there a room that costs about $60 a night?
有沒有一晚60塊美金左右的客房？

⓬ Does the price include breakfast? 費用有含早餐嗎？

room with a balcony 有陽台的房間

bayview suite 灣景套房

---

⑬ Does that include tax and service charges?
費用包含稅及服務費嗎？

---

⑭ Do you have any cheaper rooms? 有沒有便宜一點的房間？

---

⑮ I'd like a room with a nice view. 我要一間視野比較好的房間。

---

⑯ I'd like a quiet room. 麻煩給我一間比較安靜的房間。

---

⑰ I'll take that room. 我要訂那個房間。

---

⑱ What time can I check in? 我什麼時候可以辦住宿手續？

---

2 辦理住宿登記

⑲ I'd like to check in, please. 我要辦理住宿手續。

---

⑳ My name is Jeremy Wilson. I have a reservation.
我叫傑洛米‧威爾森，我有訂房。

㉑ I have a 3-day reservation starting today.
我訂了三天的房間，從今天開始算起。

㉒ I've reserved a superior suite. 我訂了一間高級套房。

23 I made a reservation in Taiwan. 我已經在台灣訂好房間了。

24 Here is my confirmation slip. 這是訂房的確認書。

25
Ⓐ I'm sorry, we don't have your reservation.

Ⓑ I'm sure I have a reservation. Can you try to find my name again?

Ⓐ 抱歉，我們的訂房單上沒有您的名字。

Ⓑ 我確定我有訂房，可以請你再找找看是否有我的名字？

26 I don't have a reservation. Is there a room available tonight? 我沒有訂房，請問今晚還有空房嗎？

27 I'd like a single room for two nights.
請給我一間單人房，要住兩晚。

28 I'm sorry, but we are full. 抱歉，我們已經客滿了。

29 Unfortunately, all the singles are booked. But we still have a few doubles left.
抱歉，單人房都已經客滿了，我們只剩下幾間雙人房。

30 How much is the room charge? 房間的費用是多少？

31 Would you fill out this registration card? 請填寫住宿單。

32 When is checkout time? 退房的時間是幾點？

33 Will you carry my luggage to my room?
你可以幫我把行李搬到房間去嗎？

3 櫃台

34 Will you keep my valuables? 可以幫我保管貴重物品嗎？

35 Can you tell me how to use the safety box?
可以告訴我保險箱的使用方法嗎？

36 Where is the emergency exit? 緊急逃生門在哪裡？

37 Where is the dining room? 餐廳在哪裡？

38 What time does breakfast start? 早餐幾點開始？

39 Will you keep my key? 可以幫我保管鑰匙嗎？

40 May I have the key to room 215? 可以給我215號房的鑰匙嗎？

41 Please airmail this letter. 請幫我把這封信用航空郵件寄出。

42 I'd like to send a fax to Taiwan. 我想傳真到台灣。

43 Are there any messages for me? 有沒有我的留言？

44 Can you tell me how to use the housephone?
可以告訴我內線電話的使用方法嗎？

elevator 電梯

emergency exit 緊急逃生門

4 客房服務

45 This is Room Service. May I help you?
這裡是客房服務中心，有什麼能為您服務的嗎？

46 This is room 1126. I'd like to order a ham sandwich and a cup of coffee.
這是1126號房，請幫我送來一份火腿三明治和一杯咖啡。

47 I'd like to order breakfast for tomorrow.
我想訂明天的早餐。

48 Please bring some ice and water. 請幫我送冰塊和水。

49 Please bring me a blanket. 請幫我送一條毛毯。

50 I'd like a bath towel. 我想要一條浴巾。

51 This is room 807. Would you give me a wake-up call?
這裡是807號房，可以請你給我morning call嗎？

52 Would you give me a wake-up call at 7 a.m.?
明天早上7點可以請你給我morning call嗎？

No Smoking 禁止吸菸

Swimming Pool 游泳池

z z z
PLEASE
DO NOT
DISTURB

DO NOT DISTURB
請勿打擾

PLEASE
MAKE UP
ROOM

MAKE UP ROOM
請打掃房間

Laundry Room 洗衣房

5 洗衣服務

53 I have some laundry. Do you have laundry service?
我有要清洗的衣物，請問有洗衣的服務嗎？

54
Ⓐ When will it be ready?
Ⓑ By tomorrow evening.
Ⓐ 什麼時候可以洗好？
Ⓑ 明天晚上。

55 Can you clean my suit for me by tomorrow morning?
明天早上以前可以幫我把西裝洗好嗎？

56 I need to have my laundry done as quickly as possible.
我的衣物需要盡速送洗。

6 住宿時遇到的麻煩 043

57 This is not the room I asked for. 這和我想訂的房間不一樣。

58 The room next door is too noisy. 隔壁的房間很吵。

59 I'd like to get a different room, please. 我想換房間。

60 The room light doesn't work. 房間的電燈壞了。

61 Something's wrong with the air conditioner. 空調有問題。

62 I can't get any hot water in the bathroom. 浴室沒有熱水。

63 The toilet doesn't flush. 馬桶的水沖不出來。

64 The toilet seems to be blocked. 馬桶好像阻塞了。

65 My room hasn't been cleaned. 我的房間還沒打掃。

66 There are no bath towels. 沒有浴巾。

67 I've locked myself out. 我忘記帶鑰匙了。

68 I lost the room key. 我把鑰匙弄丟了。

7 退房的說法 (044)

69 I'm going to leave tomorrow morning. 我明天早上離開。

70 I'd like to stay one more night. 我想再多住一晚。

71 I'm going to leave early tomorrow morning. Please have my bill ready. 我明天一早要離開，所以請先準備好帳單。

72 I'd like to check out now. Can you take my luggage down? 我現在要辦退房，可以麻煩你把我的行李拿下來嗎？

73 I'd like to check out, please. 我要辦退房。

74 My bill, please. 麻煩幫我結帳。

75 I had two bottles of beer and a cola from the refrigerator. 我喝了冰箱裡的兩瓶啤酒和一瓶可樂。

76 What's this charge for? 這是什麼費用？

77 I think there's a mistake in this bill. 這帳單好像算錯了。

78 Do you accept traveler's checks? 可以用旅行支票嗎？

79 Can I pay by credit card? 可以用信用卡付款嗎？

80 Can you keep my luggage until five o'clock? 可以幫我保管行李到五點嗎？

81 I left something in my room. 我有東西放在房間裡忘記拿了。

82 Will you call me a cab, please? 可以幫我叫輛計程車嗎？

6 餐廳
RESTAURANTS

DIALOGUE 1

May I Take Your Order? 請問您要點菜了嗎?

A　May I take your order?

B　A beer, steak with French fries, and the chef's special salad.

A　How would you like your steak?

B　Well-done, please.

A　Yes. And what kind of dressing on your salad?

B　Thousand Island dressing, please.

A　請問您要點菜了嗎?

B　我要一瓶啤酒、牛排、薯條和主廚沙拉。

A　請問牛排要幾分熟?

B　我要全熟的。

A　好的。那麼請問沙拉醬要用哪一種醬?

B　請給我千島醬。

Study Points

May I take your order?	決定要點什麼了嗎？	這是服務生詢問客人點餐時的常用説法
How would you like your steak?	您的牛排要幾分熟？	「How would you like . . .」用來詢問對食物的喜好或品嚐結果
Well-done, please.	我要全熟的。	well-done 指「全熟」
What kind of dressing on your salad?	您要哪一種沙拉醬？	常見的沙拉醬有法式沙拉醬、義式沙拉醬和千島醬等

到國外旅行，令人期待的活動之一就是「用餐」了。如果你只是一直擔心自己會不會點餐，不知道要怎麼吃異國料理，或是用餐禮節應該如何等等，那就無法盡情享受異國風味的美食了。

為了能有個美好的用餐經驗，我們先來學習餐飲方面的基本用語吧。在餐廳裡，如果不知道該如何點餐，不妨直接問服務生：

What do you recommend? 有什麼要推薦的餐點呢？

What's today's special? 今天的特餐是什麼？

如果已經準備好點餐，你可以説：

I'll have . . . 我想要點⋯⋯

I'll take . . . 我想要點⋯⋯

I'd like . . . 我想要點⋯⋯

. . ., please. 請給我⋯⋯

DIALOGUE 2

How Would You Like to Pay? 您想用什麼方式付款？

Ⓐ　Excuse me, can I have the bill, please?

Ⓑ　Of course. How would you like to pay, sir?

Ⓐ　What forms of payment do you accept?

Ⓑ　We accept payment by cash, credit card, and several digital wallet services.

Ⓐ　In that case, I'll pay with my phone. Do you accept Apple Pay?

Ⓑ　We do. Wait a moment, please. I'll be right back.

Ⓐ　不好意思，我要買單。

Ⓑ　好的，先生，您想用什麼方式付款？

Ⓐ　你們接受什麼付款方式？

Ⓑ　我們接受現金、刷卡，還有幾家數位支付服務。

Ⓐ　這樣的話，我要用手機付款。你們接受 Apple Pay嗎？

Ⓑ　有的，請稍等一下，我隨即回來。

pay with your phone
手機付款

Study Points

have the bill	結帳	也可說「have the check」。
forms of payment	付款方式	form 在此為「方式」之意。
payment by . . .	透過……付款	「透過……付款」的介系詞為 by。
in that case	那樣的話	前面已說明某種情況，此句表示「依據該情況」。
wait a moment	等一下	同樣說法還有「wait a second」。

如何使用行動支付 How to pay with your mobile phone

① Add your credit card to your payment-enabled mobile phone or device.
在你的手機或行動裝置綁定信用卡。

② Look for the contactless symbol on the terminal at checkout.
在結帳櫃檯尋找感應圖示。

③ Hold your phone or device over the symbol to pay.
將手機或裝置放置於圖示上方感應付款。

> 註：此種感應支付之手機需支援 NFC 功能，
> 透過 NFC 感應支付的有
> Apple Pay、Samsung Pay 與 Android Pay。

Table Etiquette
餐桌禮儀

勿擅自自行入內

- 進入餐廳大廳之後，不要隨便地走進去，要先告訴入口處的服務人員，說明你是否有事先訂位以及用餐人數，等服務人員安排好位子之後再進去。
- 入座時，要用右手拉椅子，並從左側入座。

用餐時的禮儀

- 喝湯時勿出聲。即使湯很燙，也不要做出把湯吹冷的樣子。
- 不要一邊吃東西，一邊說話。
- 勿將盤子舉起或是靠在嘴上。
- 刀、叉若是掉在地上，可請服務生幫忙撿起來，不要自己去撿。
- 避免討論低俗的話題。
- 如果你拿不到鹽或是胡椒時，可以跟坐在附近的人說：「Pass me the salt, please.」請他們幫忙傳遞，不要自己伸手去拿。
- 不要互相分菜。

刀叉的使用順序

- 餐桌上的刀叉是依照上菜順序由外向內排列的，所以使用的順序也是一樣，先從最外面的餐具開始使用。
- 用餐中若想將刀、叉放在餐盤上，以「八」字型擺放，結束用餐時則一律靠右排放。

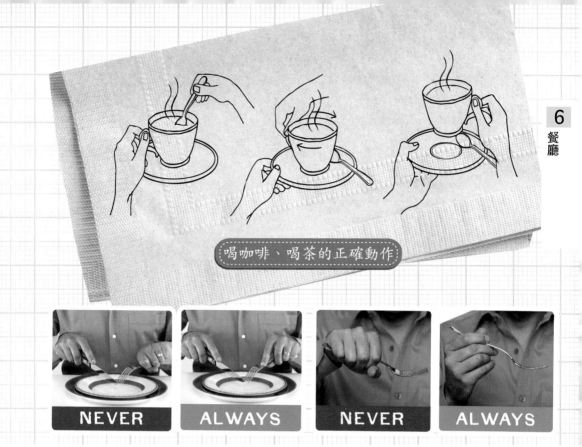

喝咖啡、喝茶的正確動作

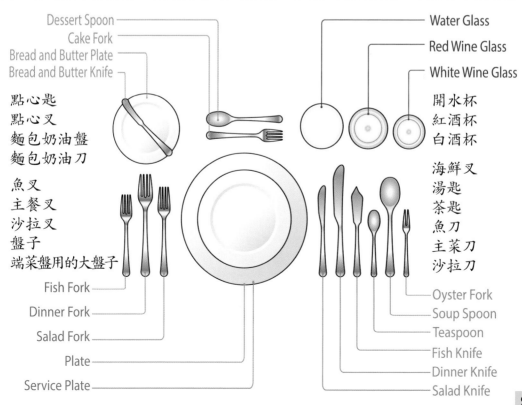

NEVER　　ALWAYS　　NEVER　　ALWAYS

Dessert Spoon
Cake Fork
Bread and Butter Plate
Bread and Butter Knife

點心匙
點心叉
麵包奶油盤
麵包奶油刀

魚叉
主餐叉
沙拉叉
盤子
端菜盤用的大盤子

Fish Fork
Dinner Fork
Salad Fork
Plate
Service Plate

Water Glass
Red Wine Glass
White Wine Glass

開水杯
紅酒杯
白酒杯

海鮮叉
湯匙
茶匙
魚刀
主菜刀
沙拉刀

Oyster Fork
Soup Spoon
Teaspoon
Fish Knife
Dinner Knife
Salad Knife

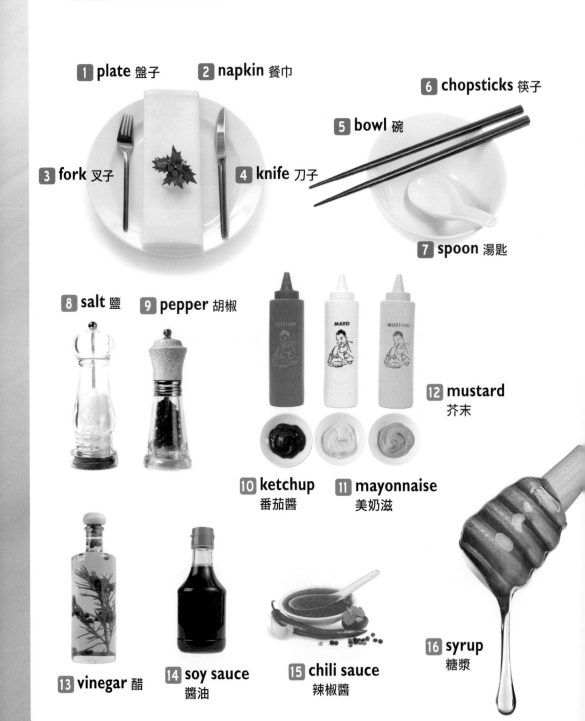

1 **plate** 盤子　　2 **napkin** 餐巾

6 **chopsticks** 筷子

5 **bowl** 碗

3 **fork** 叉子　　4 **knife** 刀子

7 **spoon** 湯匙

8 **salt** 鹽　　9 **pepper** 胡椒

12 **mustard** 芥末

10 **ketchup** 番茄醬　　11 **mayonnaise** 美奶滋

16 **syrup** 糖漿

13 **vinegar** 醋　　14 **soy sauce** 醬油　　15 **chili sauce** 辣椒醬

果醬

jam：由整顆果醬製成，有果粒

jelly：由果汁製成，質地較稀，無果粒

6
餐廳

VOCABULARY

17 peanut butter 花生醬

18 jelly 果醬

19 beef 牛肉

20 lamb 羊肉

21 pork 豬肉

22 chicken 雞肉

23 sausage 香腸

24 seafood 海鮮

25 pasta 義大利麵　　**26** pizza 比薩　　**27** fast food 速食

28 panfry 煎　　**29** deep-fry 炸　　**30** sauté 炒

31 boil 煮　　**32** stew 燉　　**33** roast 烤

RESTAURANT SIGNS
餐廳招牌

cafeteria 自助餐廳

bar & restaurant 酒吧餐廳

fast food 中式快餐店

buffet 歐式自助餐廳

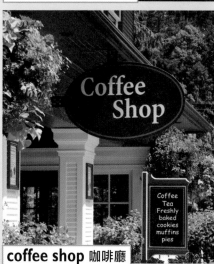

coffee shop 咖啡廳

stop and eat here!
聞香下馬，入內享用！

spaghetti with meat sauce
義大利肉醬麵

1 找餐廳 048

❶ Can you recommend a good restaurant near here?
可以推薦我這附近好吃的餐廳嗎？

❷ Where can I find the best local food?
在哪裡可以吃到好吃的當地料理呢？

❸ I'd like to try a typical dish of this country.
我想吃這個國家特有的菜。

❹ Are there any seafood restaurants around here?
這附近有海鮮餐廳嗎？

❺ Do you know of any nice, inexpensive restaurants?
你知道哪裡有好吃又便宜的餐廳嗎？

❻ I'd like a good restaurant with reasonable prices.
我想找價格合理又好吃的餐廳。

❼ I'd like to have some real Italian food.
我想吃點道地的義大利菜。

Italian food 義大利菜

一般正式的西餐廳，套餐的程序大約是：

點菜需要花一點時間，如果對菜單有任何不清楚的地方，可以請教服務生。同時，也要注意小費是否已包含在帳單裡。

1 Appetizer 開胃菜 → 2 Soup 湯 → 3 Salad 沙拉

6 Beverages 飲料 ← 5 Dessert 甜點 ← 4 Main dish (entrée) 主菜

2 訂位與服裝規定 049

8
- Ⓐ I'd like to reserve a table for two at seven tonight.
- Ⓑ I'm sorry, but it's full at that time. Can you make it at 8:00?
- Ⓐ I'm afraid I can't. Thank you, anyway.
- Ⓐ 我想訂今天晚上七點、兩個人的位子。
- Ⓑ 很抱歉，那個時段已經客滿了，請問您要不要訂八點的呢？
- Ⓐ 我恐怕不行，還是謝謝你。

9 I'd like to make a reservation, please. 我要訂位。

10 Do I have to be formally dressed? 一定要穿正式的服裝嗎？

11 Should I wear a tie? 需要打領帶嗎？

12 The name is Lin. We have a reservation for 7 o'clock.
訂位姓氏是林，我們訂了七點的位子。

---

13 We don't have a reservation. Do you have a table for four?
我們沒有訂位，請問有四個人的位子嗎？

---

14 Can we have a table? 有空位嗎？

15

(A) I'd like a table for three, please.

(B) Sorry, but our tables are full now.
Can you wait for a while?

(A) About how long do we have to wait?

(B) I think it's about 30 minutes.

(A) All right. We'll wait.

(A) 我要三個人的位子。

(B) 很抱歉，目前剛好客滿，
可以請您稍等一會嗎？

(A) 大概要等多久呢？

(B) 大約30分鐘左右。

(A) 好吧，我們要等。

---

16 May we wait for a table? 我們可以等位子嗎？

---

17 Are you serving lunch now? 現在開始供應午餐了嗎？

---

18 Can we have a table by the window?
我們可以坐靠窗的位子嗎？

---

19 We'd like seats near the street. 我們想要靠街道的位子。

4 點餐 (051)

20 Excuse me. May I see the menu? 不好意思，請給我看菜單。

21 Would you show me a wine list? 請給我看酒類的菜單。

22 What do you recommend? 你推薦什麼菜色？

23 What's today's special? 今天的特餐是什麼？

24 Which dish does the chef recommend?
主廚推薦的料理是哪一個？

25 ① Do you have a table d'hôte?
② Do you have the fixed meal of the day? 有套餐嗎？

26 What can you serve quickly? 有什麼是可以立刻上菜的？

27 What is this like? （指著菜單）這是什麼料理？

28 What kind of drinks do you have? 有哪些飲料？

29 What kind of drinks do you have for an aperitif?
有什麼餐前酒？

30 Do you have a house wine? 有自釀酒嗎？

31 Excuse me. May I order now? 不好意思，我要點餐。

32 I'm ready to order. 我要點餐。

33 I'll start with a beer. 請先給我一杯啤酒。

34 A bottle of red wine, please. 麻煩給我一瓶紅酒。

35
- Ⓐ May I take your order?
- Ⓑ Just a moment, please. I haven't decided yet.
- Ⓐ 決定好要點餐了嗎？
- Ⓑ 請等一下，我還沒決定好。

36
- Ⓐ Are you ready to order?
- Ⓑ Let me think for a moment.
- Ⓐ 決定好要點餐了嗎？
- Ⓑ 請讓我考慮一下。

37 I'll have this and this. （指著菜單）請給我這個和這個。

38 I'll have the same. 我也點跟他（指同行者）一樣的。

39 Can I have the same dish that he is having?
（指著別桌的菜）請給我跟他一樣的菜。

40 I'll take today's special. 我要點今天的特餐。

41 How would you like your steak? 請問牛排要幾分熟？

42 I'd like a seafood salad. 請給我一盤海鮮沙拉。

43 I'll start with chicken consommé. 麻煩先給我清燉雞湯。

44 I'll have the sirloin steak with mashed potatoes.
麻煩給我沙朗牛排加馬鈴薯泥。

45 What's the garnish? 食物上裝飾的是什麼？

46

Ⓐ What kind of dressing would you like on your salad?

Ⓑ Thousand Island dressing, please.

Ⓐ 請問您的生菜沙拉要加哪一種醬？

Ⓑ 請給我千島沙拉醬。

47 I'll have coffee after dinner. 餐後請給我咖啡。

48 I'd like ice cream for dessert. 餐後點心我要點冰淇淋。

49 I'll order dessert later. 餐後點心我待會兒再點。

50 I'll pass on the dessert. 餐後點心不用了。

rare 一分熟	medium-rare 三分熟	medium 五分熟	medium-well 七分熟	well-done 全熟
僅牛排的表面煎熟呈褐色，內裡的肉微暖，呈血紅色，刀切下時會有帶點血水。	牛排的表面呈褐色，中間部分的肉溫溫的，呈紅色。	牛排外圍呈褐色，中間的肉呈粉紅色，中心部分溫熱，但仍可見一絲絲血紅色。	中間部分的肉呈褐色，中心溫熱，外圍成稍暗紅色，中心部分略呈現粉紅色。	整塊牛排完全熟透，並稍微烤焦。無血水，只有肉汁，肉呈淡褐色。

5 用餐 🎧052

51 May I change my order? 我可以更改已點的餐點嗎？

52 My order hasn't come yet. 我點的東西還沒來耶。

53 I didn't order this. 我沒有點這個。

54 This is not what I ordered. 這和我點的東西不一樣。

55 I'm afraid this is a little undercooked. 這個好像沒熟。

56 I dropped a fork. May I have another one?
我的叉子掉了，可以再給我一支新的叉子嗎？

57 Can you bring me the pepper? 可以幫我拿胡椒粉過來嗎？

58 Can you pass me the salt?
（對別的客人說）可以請您把鹽遞給我嗎？

59 Can I have a glass of water? 可以給我一杯水嗎？

60 May I see the menu again? 可以再給我一次菜單嗎？

61 I'd like to have more bread, please. 請再給我一些麵包。

62 I'd like another beer, please. 請再給我一瓶啤酒。

63 Take this away, please. 請把這個收走。

64 Can I take this home? 我可以把這個打包回家嗎？

65 May I have a doggy bag? 請給我打包用的袋子。

6　結帳付款

66　May I have my bill, please? 我要結帳。

67　Can I pay at the table? 我可以直接在這裡桌邊結帳嗎？

68　Where is the cashier? 收銀台在哪裡？

69　Separate checks, please. 我們要各付各的。

70　Let's split it today. 今天各付各的。

71　I'll take care of the bill. 由我來付。

72　① This is my treat.
　　② This is on me. 這次我請客。

73　How much is it altogether? 總共多少錢？

74　Does that include the tip? 有含服務費嗎？

75　I think there's a mistake in the bill. 這帳單好像算錯了。

76　Can I pay with this credit card? 可以用這張卡付款嗎？

77　Can I have a receipt? 可以給我收據嗎？

在美國，餐廳用餐的服務費並不像台灣直接附加於餐點費用上，而是要直接給服務生小費（**tip**）。午餐的**小費**通常是 10% ～ 15%；晚餐則是 15% ～ 20%；高級餐廳則可能到 20% ～ 25%。

另外，餐廳用餐時，每桌通常會有固定的服務生，在最一開始會先自我介紹，用餐時需要認一下自己的服務生，亂叫別的服務生可能會被視為不禮貌的行為。

7　速食、簡餐

78　Two hamburgers and two small colas, please.
我要兩個漢堡和兩杯小可。

79　Will you be eating here? 您要內用嗎？

80　
Ⓐ　(Is this) For here or to go?
Ⓑ　For here, please.
Ⓐ　內用，還是外帶呢？
Ⓑ　我要內用。

81　I'd like carryout [takeout]. 我要外帶。

82　Would you like ketchup or mustard on that?
請問要加番茄醬，還是芥末醬嗎？

83　
Ⓐ　How would you like your eggs?
Ⓑ　Sunny-side up, please.
Ⓐ　請問您的蛋要多熟？
Ⓑ　我要只煎一面的不熟荷包蛋。

84　I'd like a cup of coffee and a pancake. 請給我咖啡和鬆餅。

85　
Ⓐ　Cream and sugar?
Ⓑ　Just cream, please.
Ⓐ　要加奶精和糖嗎？
Ⓑ　只要加奶精就好了。

hard-boiled egg
全熟水煮蛋

medium-boiled egg
半熟水煮蛋

soft-boiled egg
不熟水煮蛋

sunny-side up
只煎一面
蛋黃不熟

over easy
兩面都煎
蛋黃不熟

over medium
兩面都煎
蛋黃半熟

over hard
兩面都煎
蛋黃全熟

scrambled eggs
炒蛋

omelet
西式蛋餅

poached egg
無殼水波蛋

8 酒吧

86 Is there room at the counter? 吧檯有空位嗎？

87 What would you like to drink? 請問要喝什麼嗎？

88 Whiskey and water, please. 請給我威士忌加水。

89 I'd like a Scotch on the rocks. 請給我蘇格蘭酒加冰塊。

90 Give us three shots of bourbon, please.
麻煩給我們三杯波本威士忌。

91 Two beers, please. 請給我兩瓶啤酒。

92
Ⓐ What brand?
Ⓑ Budweiser, please.
Ⓐ 要點什麼牌子的？
Ⓑ 請給我一瓶百威。

93 What's your special cocktail? 你們的特調雞尾酒是哪一種？

94 I'll have a martini. 我要一杯馬丁尼。

95 Do you have any snacks? 有點心嗎？

96 May I have another one, please? 請再給我一杯。

97 I'll buy you a drink. 我請你喝一杯。

DIFFERENT WINE GLASSES
各種酒杯介紹

tumbler
平底無腳酒杯

goblet
高腳杯

beer mug
啤酒杯

white wine glass
白葡萄酒酒杯

red wine glass
紅葡萄酒酒杯

shot of vodka
伏特加酒杯

whiskey glass
威士忌酒杯

brandy glass
白蘭地酒杯

sherry glass
雪莉酒酒杯

champagne flute
笛型香檳杯

champagne saucer
寬底香檳杯

highball glass
高球杯
（海波杯）

Collins glass
可林杯

old-fashioned glass
古典杯

cocktail glass
雞尾酒杯

7 購物
SHOPPING

DIALOGUE 1

How Much Is This Blouse? 這件襯衫多少錢？ (056)

A I'm looking for a blouse. How much is this blouse?

B It's on sale now for just $30.49.

A May I try it on?

B Sure. The fitting room is over there. . . . How is it?

A I like this, but it's a bit too big. Do you have a smaller one?

B Yes, we do. Here you are.

A This fits perfectly. I'll take it.

A 我想買襯衫。請問這件要多少錢？

B 這件正在打折，打完折後是30.49美元。

A 我可以試穿嗎？

B 可以，試衣間在那裡。……穿起來感覺怎麼樣？

A 我很喜歡，但是它稍微大了一點。有再小一點的嗎？

B 有的，在這兒。

A 這件剛剛好，我要買這件。

Study Points

It's on sale.	特價中	「出售中」是 for sale
May I try it on?	可以試穿嗎？	try on 是「試穿」
Do you have a smaller one?	有小一號的嗎？	相反句是：Do you have a bigger one?（有大一號的嗎？）
This fits perfectly.	這件剛剛好。	衣服、首飾或鞋子，都可以用這句話來表達尺寸適合
I'll take this.	我要買這個。	take 是「買下」

「購物」是海外旅行的一項樂趣，在出發購物之前，最好先調查大型的購物中心、百貨公司和大賣場等的種種情報，因為歐美有許多商店在星期天都是不營業的。這方面的資料也可以向旅客服務中心，或是飯店櫃檯洽詢。

在國外逛街買衣服，走進商店時，店員通常都會走過來親切地和你打招呼，問你：

May I help you? 需要幫忙嗎？
What can I do for you? 有什麼可以幫忙的嗎？
Are you looking for something? 您想找什麼商品嗎？

如果你只是想逛逛而已，就可以客氣地跟她說聲：

I'm just looking. 我只是看看而已。
I'm just browsing. 我只是逛逛而已。

海外旅行的一大樂趣，就是找到國內沒有賣的物品，或是買到比國內還要便宜的東西，甚至可以要求店員打折，充分享受購物殺價的樂趣，你可以用英語對店員說：

Can you give me a discount? 可以算便宜一點嗎？

在歐洲，因為有免稅制度，所以可以退還稅金。以英國為例，除了免稅商店之外，外國旅客在其他商店，只要購買一定的金額，就會被要求加上**額外的稅金（VAT, Value Add Tax）**，但只要透過一些手續，這些外加的稅金還是可以退還回來的。例如，英國的 VAT 是 20%，但是每個國家的 VAT 匯率都不一樣，所以最好事先調查清楚。如果你要辦理退稅的話，那付款前就要先跟店員說：

I'd like to buy it under the value added tax system.
我買這個想退稅金。

出示護照和機票之後，店方會把印有這家店名的信封和相關表格交給你，你只要在出境的時候，將護照及表格拿給海關人員檢查，如果沒問題的話，海關人員就會在表格上蓋章，然後你就可以到機場的退稅窗口辦理退稅手續，這樣就可以領到退稅的錢了。

如果你是在無法退現金的國家退稅，那就只要把表格放進信封內，並在海關處投至專用的信箱裡，回國之後就可以領到退稅的金額了。至於退款的方式是要郵寄支票，還是匯到信用卡的戶頭裡，這在你申請退稅的表格上就得先選好了。

像美國對國外的旅客就沒有免稅的制度，因為各州的稅率不同，所以在稅金較低的州購買比較划算喔！

SENTENCE PATTENRNS
句型練習

a pair of sneakers

a pair of glasses

a sweater

some dresses

some shirts

我想買……

I'm looking for . . .

I'd like . . .

I'd like to buy . . .

I want to buy . . .

\+

ACCESSORIES

TOPS

SKIRTS & DRESSES

TROUSERS

HEELS

ACCESSORY	配件
SKIRT	短裙
DRESS	洋裝
HEELS	高跟鞋
TOP	上衣
TROUSERS	褲子

1 shopping center 購物中心

2 department store 百貨公司

3 supermarket 超市

4 convenience store 便利商店

5 drugstore 藥妝店

6 cashier 收銀台

7 **escalator** 電扶梯

8 **elevator** 電梯

9 **window** 櫥窗

10 **cart** 購物推車

11 **on sale** 特價中

12 **discount** 折扣

1 尋找商店或賣場

❶ Is there a department store around here?
這附近有百貨公司嗎？

❷ Where's the most famous department store?
最有名的百貨公司在哪裡？

❸ Can you tell me where the nearest shopping area is?
可以告訴我最近的商店街在哪裡嗎？

❹ Is there a duty-free shop near here?
這附近有免稅商店嗎？

❺ Is there a souvenir shop around here?
這附近有販賣紀念品的商店嗎？

❻ Where is the drugstore? 藥妝店在哪裡呢？

❼ Where is the nearest supermarket?
離這裡最近的超市在哪裡？

❽ Where's the ladies' department? 女裝部在哪裡？

❾ Where's the bookstore? 書店在哪裡？

2 選購與採買

10
- Ⓐ Hello. May I help you?
- Ⓑ I'm looking for a sweater.
- Ⓐ 歡迎光臨。請問您需要什麼嗎？
- Ⓑ 我要找毛衣。

---

11 I'd like to see some watches. 我想看手錶。

---

12 Which brand do you recommend?
請問哪個牌子比較好？

---

13 I want to buy some lipstick. Do you have Revlon products?
我想買口紅，有露華濃的牌子嗎？

---

14 May I look at this? 我可以看一下這個嗎？

---

15 Will you show me something else? 還有沒有別的樣式？

---

16 I'd like to see this in a different fabric.
我想看看別種紋路的。

---

17 Do you have one that's a little bigger?
有沒有大一點的？

---

18 Do you have anything cheaper? 有沒有更便宜一點的？

---

19 What is this made of? 這是什麼材質做的？

---

20 Is this made of leather? 這是真皮的嗎？

3 詢問價錢與殺價

21 How much is it? 多少錢？

22 How much does it cost? 多少錢？

23 How much is it altogether? 全部多少錢？

24 How much for one? 一個多少錢？

25 What's the price [cost] of this bag? 這個皮包多少錢？

26 Does the price include tax? 這個價格含稅嗎？

27 That's too expensive. 那太貴了。

28 Could you give me a discount? 可以打個折嗎？

29 Can't you make it a little cheaper? 可以再算便宜一點嗎？

國外觀光區的商品定價通常偏高，遊客向老闆殺價或討折扣，幾乎是不可避免的過程。但若是商家已在門口或牆壁貼上 Fixed Price（不二價），表示不願意降價，遊客就不應該再開口殺價，以免顯得不禮貌，成為不受歡迎的奧客。

折扣

新品

打折價　特價

新貨　熱賣

4 購買與否、付款和包裝

30 I like this. I'll take it. 這個不錯，我要這個。

31 I can't find what I want. 我找不到想買的東西。

32 Can I pay by traveler's check?
可以使用旅行支票付帳嗎？

33 Do you take MasterCard? 你們收萬事達卡嗎？

34 Can I have a receipt, please? 請給我收據。

35 I'm afraid I was shortchanged.
你們找的零錢好像不夠。

36 Would you wrap it, please?
可以幫我包裝嗎？

37 Please wrap it up. 請幫我包裝。

38 Will you wrap these separately, please?
請分開包裝，好嗎？

在國外若是看到 20% OFF、30% OFF 這種標示，就代表商品正在打折。
OFF 有「去掉」的意思，30% OFF 就代表拿掉原定價錢的 30%，還剩 70%，也就是打七折。

5 買衣服 🎧062

39 I want a jacket. 我想買外套。

40 Can you show me the sweater in the window?
可以給我看櫥窗裡的毛衣嗎？

41
- Ⓐ What size do you wear?
- Ⓑ I'm not sure. Can you take my measurements?
- Ⓐ 您是穿幾號的？
- Ⓑ 我不太清楚耶，可以幫我量嗎？

42 What is this made of? 這件衣服的材質是什麼？

43 May I try it on? 可以試穿嗎？

44 May I try this jacket on? 這件夾克可以試穿嗎？

45 Where's the fitting room? 試衣間在哪裡？

46 It's too small for me. Do you have a larger one?
這件太小了，有更大一點的嗎？

47 It's too loose. 這件太鬆了。

48 It's a little tight in the waist. 腰的地方有點緊。

49 This fits me perfectly. 這件剛剛好。

50 This is too loud for me. Do you have a plain one?
這件對我來說太豔了，有沒有素一點的？

51 Can you show me one in a lighter color?
可以讓我看看稍微淡一點的顏色嗎？

52 Do you have any other styles? 還有其他款式嗎？

53 Is this washable? 這件可以水洗嗎？

54 Will this shrink if it's washed in cold water?
這件用冷水洗的話會縮水嗎？

55 Will you adjust the length? 可以修改長度嗎？

6 買貴金屬飾品

56 Will you show me that ring, please?
可以給我看那枚戒指嗎？

57 The second one from the right. 從右邊數過來的第二個。

58　Ⓐ What kind of stone is this?
　　Ⓑ It's an opal.
　　Ⓐ 這是什麼寶石？
　　Ⓑ 這是貓眼石。

opal 貓眼石

59 I'd like to see some ruby rings. 我想看紅寶石的戒指。

60 How many karats is this?
這個幾克拉？

127

pierced earrings
穿耳式耳環

ear clip earrings
耳夾式耳環

61

Ⓐ **Is this necklace gold?**

Ⓑ **Yes, 18-karat gold.**

Ⓐ 這條項鍊是金的嗎？

Ⓑ 是的，它是18K金的。

62 **Do you have pierced earrings?** 有穿耳的耳環嗎？

63 **Does it come with a guarantee?** 有附保證書嗎？

7 買鞋的用語

64 **I want some black leather shoes.** 我想買黑色皮鞋。

65 **What sort of leather is this?** 這是什麼皮做的？

66 **I'd like to try on these shoes.** 我想試穿這雙鞋。

67 **I'm not sure of my size.** 我不知道我的尺寸。

68 **Do you have these same shoes one size larger?**
這個款式有再大一號的嗎？

69 **This pair fits me perfectly.** 這雙很合腳。

70 **Do you have the same size in red?**
同樣大小的有紅色的嗎？

8　買化妝品

71　Do you carry Chanel perfumes? 你們有賣香奈兒的香水嗎？

72　What's a popular perfume? 哪一種香水最暢銷？

73　I want eau de cologne. 我想買古龍水。

74　I want to buy a lipstick. I'd like a rose color.
　　我想買口紅，要玫瑰色系的。

75　I'd like to try this lipstick color. 我想試這個顏色的口紅。

76　Do you have any lighter colors? 有再淡一點的顏色嗎？

77　Please show me some nail polish. 請給我看指甲油。

78　Do you have a foundation for summer?
　　有夏天用的粉底嗎？

blush 粉餅

powder puff 粉撲

foundation 粉底

brush 粉刷

mascara 睫毛膏

lipstick 口紅

8 郵局
POST OFFICE

DIALOGUE 1
Sending Mail 寄送郵件

Ⓐ I'd like to send this letter to Taiwan.

Ⓑ Airmail or sea mail?

Ⓐ How long will it take by airmail?

Ⓑ It should take four or five days by regular airmail and two or three days by special delivery.

Ⓐ Then send it by special delivery, please. And I'd like 20 of the 50-cent stamps.

Ⓑ That'll be $12.30, please.

Ⓐ 我想寄這封信到台灣。

Ⓑ 你要寄航空的，還是海運？

Ⓐ 寄航空信多久會到呢？

Ⓑ 普通郵件是四到五天，快捷郵件則是二到三天會到。

Ⓐ 那我要寄快捷郵件。另外，我還要買20張50分錢的郵票。

Ⓑ 這樣總共是$12.30。

Study Points

send this letter	寄這封信	信件的英文，美式是 mail，英式是 post
Airmail or sea mail?	要寄航空還是海運？	海運也可以説 surface mail
How long will it take?	要花多久的時間？	花費多少時間，動詞要用 take
by special delivery	快遞	快遞也可以説 express delivery 或 express mail
50-cent stamps	50 分錢的郵票	量詞作形容詞時要用單數形，所以用 50-cent，而不是 50 cents

現在國際電話或手機漫遊非常方便，抵達飯店後，就可以直接打電話回國，但是如果能寄些國外的風景明信片回國，或是親自寫信給國內的友人，會別有一番情意。

在國外寄郵件，一般在明信片或是信上貼好郵票，交給飯店的櫃檯就可以。但如果要寄包裹或是掛號，那就需要跑一趟郵局囉。

1 **post office** 郵局

2 **mailbox** 郵筒

3 **stamp** 郵票

5 **letter paper** 信紙

4 **envelope** 信封

6 **postcard** 明信片

8 **sender** 寄件人

7 **parcel; package** 包裹

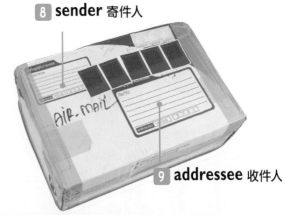

9 **addressee** 收件人

11 sea mail 海運

10 airmail 空運

12 registered mail 掛號信

13 express delivery 快捷

14 fragile; breakable 易碎的

常見的紙箱標誌

FRAGILE
易碎品

KEEP AWAY FROM WATER
避免潮濕

THIS WAY UP
向上

HANDLE WITH CARE
小心輕放

Useful Expressions

1 郵局窗口

1 Which window is for mail service?
請問寄信的窗口在哪裡？

2 Which window is for registered mail?
寄掛號信的窗口是哪一個？

3 At which window can I mail this package/parcel?
寄包裹的窗口是哪一個？

4 I'd like to send this by airmail. 這封信我要用航空郵件寄。

5 By sea mail, please. 我要寄海運。

6 I'd like to send this by express mail. 這個要寄快捷。

7 Please send this by special delivery. 這個要寄快遞。

8 Please send this letter by registered mail.
這封信要寄掛號。

9 I'd like to send this as printed matter. 這個請當印刷品寄。

10 What is the fastest way to send this?
用什麼方式寄會最快抵達？

11 I'd like to send this the quickest way.
我這個想用最快的方式寄送。

12 What is the cheapest way to send this?
哪一種郵寄方式的費用最便宜？

13 I'd like to send a money order to Honolulu.
我想寄匯票到檀香山。

14 Can I cash this postal money order?
這張郵政匯票可以換成現金嗎？

15

Ⓐ I'd like to send a package to Taiwan.

Ⓑ What's in this?

Ⓐ All clothes.

Ⓐ 我想寄包裹到台灣。

Ⓑ 這裡面裝什麼？

Ⓐ 都是衣服。

2 詢問費用

16 How much is the postage on this? 這個郵資是多少錢？

17 How much does it cost to send this package to Taiwan?
這個包裹寄到台灣要多少錢？

18 How much will it be by airmail? 寄空運要多少錢？

19 What's the registration fee? 掛號費是多少？

20 How much is it altogether? 總共是多少錢？

21 How much is the postage to Taiwan?
寄到台灣的郵資要多少錢？

22 How much will it cost to send this? 寄這個要多少郵資？

23 Twelve thirty-cent stamps, please. 我要12張30分錢的郵票。

24 I'd like five fifteen-cent stamps, ten twenty-five-cent stamps, and twenty postcards, please.
我要買5張0.15元和10張0.25元的郵票，還要20張明信片。

25 Can you give me fifteen aerograms?
我要買15張航空郵簡。

如果要從國外寄明信片或包裹回台灣，建議在出國之前，先上中華郵政的網站（http://www.post.gov.tw/post/index.jsp）查詢自己家裡的英文地址。如果已經到了國外，不知道該怎麼寫台灣的住址，那也可以用中文寫地址，最後再加上 Taiwan, R.O.C.。

3　詢問所需時間　

26 How long will it take by sea mail?
寄海運的話，要多久才會到？

27 When will it get to Taipei? 什麼時候會寄到台北？

28 How long will it take to get to Taipei? 寄到台北要多久？

29 Will it get there in one week? 一週內會到嗎？

4　其他的表達方式　

30 I'd like to have this package insured.
這個包裹我想加掛保險。

31 I'd like to insure this package for $200.
這個包裹我想保險200塊美金。

32 What is the maximum coverage? 最高的賠償金額是多少？

33 Is there a weight limit? 有重量的限制嗎？

34 Do I need to fill out a customs declaration form?
我需要填寫海關申報表嗎？

35 May I have a customs declaration form?
可以給我一張海關申報表嗎？

36 How do I fill in this declaration form?
我要怎麼填寫這張海關申報表呢？

9 交通工具
TRANSPORTATION

DIALOGUE 1

What's the Best Way to Get There?
請問要怎麼去最快呢？

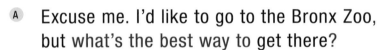

Ⓐ Excuse me. I'd like to go to the Bronx Zoo, but what's the best way to get there?

Ⓑ Let me see. You can take a bus, but the quickest way is to take the subway from here.

Ⓐ Where is the nearest subway station?

Ⓑ You can see Manhattan Station over there. The zoo is about a 10-minute walk from the East Tremont Avenue station.

Ⓐ You have been a great help. Thank you for your kindness.

Ⓐ 不好意思，我要去布隆克斯動物園，請問要怎麼去最快呢？

Ⓑ 嗯，你可以搭公車去，但是最快的方法是搭地鐵。

Ⓐ 那最近的地鐵車站在哪裡？

Ⓑ 就在那邊，那是曼哈頓站。到了東崔蒙大道站，下車再走10分鐘左右就到動物園了。

Ⓐ 你幫了我大忙，謝謝你。

Study Points

What's the best way to . . .?	去……最好的方式是什麼？	這句話是用來詢問如何抵達目的地
You can take a bus.	你可以搭公車去。	take ＋交通工具，指搭乘
Where is the nearest . . .?	最近的……在哪裡？	後面直接接地點
10-minute walk	10 分鐘的走路路程	walk 在這裡做名詞用。

一般車票都會以距離和旅遊時間來區分，以下是常見的幾種票種：

1 單程票（Single Ticket）如果只到某地，之後不會再搭車，買單程票就是最划算的選擇。

2 來回票（Return Ticket）如果回程確定了，建議在買票時就買來回票，通常比兩張單程票便宜，亦可省下再次買票的麻煩。

3 區間票 如果只在某個區域活動，可買此票種，如搭乘倫敦地鐵遊覽倫敦，就可買Zone 1與Zone 2兩區的週票，可在使用期限內於該區內任何站隨意進出。巴黎的地鐵也有此票種。

4 一日票（One-Day Pass; Daily Pass; One-Day Travel Card）如果想在某地到處觀光，一天內會不斷出入地鐵站，此票種方便又划算。

5 週票及月票（Weekly Pass & Monthly Ticket）若待在某地時間較長，可根據停留時間購買週票或月票，有的會要求附一張照片以貼在車票上。

DIALOGUE 2

Calling a Taxi With a Smartphone App 〔073〕
用手機叫計程車

A Could you **call** me a taxi?

B Do you know about our city's taxi app?

A No, I don't. Could you tell me about it?

B It's a free app that **allows** you **to** call a taxi from anywhere in the city.

A **How do I use it?**

B It's very simple. Just download the app on your smartphone.

A OK. Done.

B Now you need to enter your credit card details and destination.

A And after that?

B Just tap on "Call a Taxi" and a nearby taxi will come to **pick** you **up**.

A 妳可以幫我叫一台計程車嗎？

B 您知道我們市內的計程車叫車程式嗎？

A 不，我不知道。可以跟我說更詳細嗎？

B 這是一款免費的應用程式，可以讓您在本市內任何地方叫車。

A 要怎麼使用呢？

B 非常簡單。只要在您的智慧型手機上下載程式。

A 好，下好了。

B 接著您需要輸入信用卡資訊，與您的目的地。

A 然後呢？

B 只要按下「立即叫車」的按鈕，位於附近的計程車就會前來接您。

Study Points

call . . . a taxi	幫……叫車	幫某人叫計程車的說法。
allow . . . to . . .	允許……做……	「允許某人做某事」的介系詞為 to。
How do I use it?	我要怎麼使用它？	在不知道該如何使用某物時的詢問方法。
pick . . . up	接……	用汽車搭載或接送某人的說法。

若是使用應用程式叫計程車，通常可以在程式內輸入欲抵達的目的地，也可同時得知預估車資。但若是在路邊叫車，在招到計程車後，可先詢問司機是否知道你的目的地要怎麼去。一旦確認司機知道地址，可以請他**估價（to estimate the fare）**。最好在出發前先了解大略的車資，啟程時也要確認計程車司機有按**跳表機（taxi meter）**，抵達目的地時才不會被高昂車資嚇到，或是被司機漫天喊價。

有些國家需要給司機小費，例如在紐約，不成文的規定是要付15%到20%的小費；在其他國家，像是英國，給小費的方式則是請司機不用找零即可。

SUBWAY SYSTEM
各國地鐵

| 美國 | **Subway** | 在美國，地鐵普遍稱作Subway，但有些城市（如洛杉磯）的地鐵稱為Metro或Metro Rail。 |  |

| 英國 | **Underground/ Tube** | 英國地鐵的歷史最古老，因為在地底下如管子一般交錯，所以又稱Tube。在英國，subway是指地下道，找地鐵站時可千萬別走錯。 |  |

| 法國 | **Metro** | 一般巴黎景點都可透過Metro地鐵到達，需要注意有些列車車門不是自動，需要乘客自行按按鈕或拉桿才會開門。 |  |

| 日本 | **Subway/ Metro** | 日本許多大城市都有不同的地鐵或火車，交通方便。 |  |

| 香港 | **MTR** | 在香港搭乘地鐵時，可同時購買八達通卡，搭乘公車、渡輪、地鐵時都可使用。 |  |

DIRECTION 方向說明

1 over there 在那裡

2 next to 在……旁邊

3 in front of 在……前面

4 opposite 在……對面

5 on your right;
on the right-hand side 在右手邊

6 on your left;
on the left-hand side 在左手邊

7 behind;
at the back of 在……後面

8 at the corner of 在……轉角處

9 go straight on 直走

10 at the corner 轉角處

11 turn right 右轉

12 turn left 左轉

1 taxi stand 計程車招呼站

2 meter 計費表

3 fare（交通）費用

4 trunk 後行李廂

5 safety belt 安全帶

6 traffic lights 紅綠燈

7 intersection 十字路口

8 crosswalk 斑馬線

9 bus station 公車站　**10** railroad station 火車站　**11** route map 路線圖

12 platform 月台　**13** timetable 時刻表　**14** ticket window 售票口

15 ticket machine
自動售票機　**16** gate 剪票口　**17** conductor 列車長

Useful Expressions

1 搭計程車 (075)

1 Where is the taxi stand? 計程車招呼站在哪裡？

2 Where can I catch a taxi? 在哪裡可以招到計程車？

3 There's a taxi stand over there. 那裡有個計程車招呼站。

4 Can you call a taxi for me? 請幫我叫輛計程車，好嗎？

5
    A Where to?
    B To the Plaza Hotel, please.
    A （計程車司機）要去哪裡？
    B 到廣場飯店。

6 How long does it take to get to the airport?
到機場要多久？

7 About how much is the fare to the airport?
到機場大概要多少錢？

8 Please put this luggage in the trunk.
請把這個行李放在後車廂。

9 To the Central Hotel, please. 麻煩你到中央飯店。

10 To this address, please. 請到這個地址。

11 Please take me to this place. （給司機看地圖）請到這個地方。

TAXI FARE

$2.50	INITIAL CHARGE
40¢	Per 1/5 Mile
40¢	Per 2 Minutes Stopped/Slow Traffic
$1.00	Weekday Surcharge 4pm - 8pm
50¢	Night Surcharge 8pm - 6am

以上為一計程車費率示例，每地區里程計費標準不一，建議事前查明。

計程車計費標準

起跳費用 $2.50
續程　　 40¢／0.5 英里
延滯計時 40¢／2 分鐘

平日加成 $1.00 (4 pm - 8 pm)
夜間加成 50¢ (8 pm - 6 am)

⓬ The traffic is very heavy now. The subway would be quicker.
現在交通很擁擠，搭地鐵會比較快。

⓭ I'm in a hurry. Would you hurry, please?
我在趕時間，可以開快一點嗎？

⓮ I have to get there by six. Could you hurry along, please?
我要在六點以前到，可以請你開快一點嗎？

⓯ I've got to be at the airport by 5:30. Can we make it?
我五點半以前要到機場，來得及嗎？

⓰ Can I get to the station by 3 o'clock? 三點以前能到車站嗎？

⓱ How much longer will it take? 還要多久？

⓲ Turn to the left, please. 請往左轉。

⓳ Please stop in front of the hotel. 請在飯店前面停車。

⓴ Stop on this side of the next intersection, please.
請在下一個交叉路口靠邊停車。

21 ① Stop here, please.
② Let me off here, please. 請在這裡讓我下車。

22 ① How much is it?
② How much is the fare? 多少錢？

23 Thank you. Keep the change. 謝謝，不用找零錢了。

24 This is for you. Thank you. 謝謝，這是小費。

25 May I have a receipt? 可以給我收據嗎？

如何使用叫車應用程式
How to Use
a Taxi App

1 open your taxi app
打開叫車應用程式

2 enter username
and password
輸入帳號和密碼

3 type in address
of destination
輸入目的地地址

4 select a vehicle
option
選擇車種

5 tap "call" to
schedule a ride
按下「叫車」預訂行程

6 done 叫車完成

2 搭公車 🎧076

26 Where is the nearest bus stop? 最近的公車站牌在哪裡？

27 Do you have a bus route map? 你有公車路線圖嗎？

28 I'd like to go to Manhattan, but which bus should I take?
我想去曼哈頓，應該搭哪一路公車呢？

29 What number is the bus for Hollywood?
到好萊塢要搭幾號公車？

30 When is the next bus for Chicago?
往芝加哥的下一班公車是幾點？

31 How often do the buses run to Chicago?
往芝加哥的公車多久發車一次？

32 What time is the last bus? 末班車是幾點？

33 Does this bus go to National Airport?
這輛公車會開往國際機場嗎？

34 How much does it cost to go to Chicago?
到芝加哥要多少錢？

35 Where should I transfer to get to Soho?
去蘇活區要在哪裡轉車？

36 Where do I get off to go to City Hall?
去市政府要在哪裡下車呢？

37 I'd like to get off at Central Park. 我想在中央公園下車。

38 I'll get off at the next stop. 我下一站要下車。

39 ① I'll get off here.
② I'm getting off. 我要在這裡下車。

40 Ⓐ Am I on the bus to Chinatown?
Ⓑ ① Yes, you are.
② No, you aren't. You should get off at the next stop.
Ⓐ 這班車有到中國城嗎？
Ⓑ ① 有。
② 沒有耶，你得在下一站下車。

41 Ⓐ How many stops to Central Park?
Ⓑ It's the seventh stop.
Ⓐ 中央公園是第幾站？
Ⓑ 是第七站。

3 搭地下鐵 🎧077

42 Where is the nearest subway station?
最近的地鐵車站在哪裡？

43 May I have a subway route map?
我可以拿一份地鐵的路線圖嗎？

44 What line should I take to go to Central Park?
去中央公園要搭哪一條線呢？

45 Where do I change trains to go to Wall Street?
去華爾街要在哪裡轉車呢？

46 Where can I get a subway token?
哪裡可以買到地鐵用的代幣？

47 Where is a ticket machine? 車票的自動販賣機在哪裡？

48 How much is one token?
一枚代幣（乘車專用硬幣）多少錢？

49 Ten tokens, please. 我要十枚代幣。

50 Can I have two packs of tokens? 我要兩包代幣。

51 Does this train stop at Times Square?
這地鐵有停時代廣場嗎？

52 Which exit should I take for City Hall?
往市政府的出口是哪一個？

53 Where is the exit? 出口在哪裡？

4 搭電車或長程列車 🎧078

54 I'd like to see a timetable. 我想看時刻表。

55 Can I buy a ticket on the train? 可以在車內買票嗎？

56 A one-way ticket to Chicago, please.
我要一張到芝加哥的單程票。

57 Two round-trip tickets to Boston, please.
我要兩張到波士頓的來回票。

58 Tickets for two adults to London, please.
我要兩張到倫敦的全票。

59 Two tickets for the 2:30 express. 兩點三十分的快車票兩張。

60 How much is the fare to Chicago? 到芝加哥要多少錢？

61 What's the round-trip fare? 來回票多少錢？

62 What's the express charge? 快車票多少錢？

63 What's the sleeper fare? 臥舖車票多少錢？

64 Do I have to make a reservation for a limited express train?
特快車需要先訂位嗎？

65 I'd like to reserve a seat to Chicago. 我要訂往芝加哥的票。

66 I'd like the lower berth. 我要下舖。〔上舖是upper berth〕

67 Does the train have a dining car? 這輛車上有餐車嗎？

68 Is this the right platform for the train to Chicago?
往芝加哥的車在這個月台搭嗎？

69 Which platform should I use to take the A train?
A車在哪個月台？

70 Which track does the train to Las Vegas leave from?
前往拉斯維加斯的火車是在哪一側？

71 How many train stops to San Diego? 聖地牙哥是第幾站？

72 Is this the local or express train? 這列是普通車，還是快車？

73 Does the express train stop at Osaka? 這列快車有停大阪嗎？

74 How long does it take to get to Boston? 到波士頓要多久時間？

75 What time does this train get to L.A.? 這班車幾點到洛杉磯？

76 Where are the reserved seats? 預訂席在哪裡？

77 I took the wrong train. At which station should I get off?
我搭錯車了，要在哪一站下車才好呢？

78 At which station should I change trains?
我應該在哪一站轉車呢？

在國外旅遊時，如果想要看遍景點、又想玩得划算，那交通工具的使用就很重要。

在許多大城市都有販售組合套票，能搭乘地鐵、公車甚至遊輪；有時也有搭乘交通工具可免費參觀博物館或著名景點的套票。出國前先上網查詢或是向旅行社詢問，不但可省下一筆費用，還可看到更多景點！

搭火車旅遊是非常方便又容易的事，在歐洲大陸更為便利，可以在事前向各大旅行社購買。其中分為許多不同的票種，例如：

Eurail Pass（歐洲十七國聯營火車票）
ScanRail Pass（北歐四國聯營火車票）
Balkan Flexipass（巴爾幹半島彈性火車票）

在北美旅遊時，也有方便的火車系統可搭：

North America Rail Pass（北美聯營火車票，同時遊覽美國及加拿大）
National Rail Pass（美國火車聯票，可遊遍全美）
Northeast Rail Pass（美國東北部火車聯票，限於美國東北部）
Far West Rail Pass（美西火車聯票，限於美西）

以車程距離來區分，市區公車稱為 bus，若是**長途客運**，在美國稱 long-distance bus，在英國則稱 coach。

以公車的外型來區分，巴士可分為**單層巴士**或**雙層巴士**（double-decker）。雙層巴士是英國的「特產」，許多人到英國時，都會嚐嚐搭乘雙層巴士的滋味。

以功能來區分，除了一般的公車外，許多的大城市都有**觀光巴士**（tour bus）。觀光巴士有時也會與其他大眾運輸工具配合，買了票後，除了可以在限定的日期內自由上下車參觀名勝古蹟、著名觀光景點外，還可以搭乘其他交通工具，非常方便。

在美國，市區公車都是投幣式，車上不找零，所以上車前記得先準備一些零錢。如果是要轉乘其他巴士，司機會給一張**轉乘卡**（transfer card），這樣下段旅程將可較便宜或是免費。

在英國則相反，上車購票時司機會找零，有時可以在上車時就告知是買來回票，相對會較便宜且方便，回程上車時出示票券即可。至於長途巴士，則大多是先在站內購票後再上車。

10 租車
RENT A CAR

Renting a Car 租車

A I'd like to rent a car.

B What kind of car would you like?

A Something that is medium-sized and gets good mileage.

B Would you prefer a Japanese car?

A Something in the 2-liter class that is easy to drive and has left-hand steering.

B Why don't you try that model over there?
May I see your driver's license and credit card?

A 我要租輛車。

B 您要租什麼樣的車呢？

A 我想租比較省油的中型車。

B 您喜歡開日本車嗎？

A 只要好開就好，我要左駕的車，排氣量約2000c.c.左右。

B 那您可以試試那輛車，我可以看一下您的駕照和信用卡嗎？

Study Points

rent a car	租車	rent 是指要付費的出租
medium-sized	中型的	也可以說 middle-sized 「小型的」是 small-sized 「大型的」是 large-sized
get good mileage	省油	也可以用形容詞 economical
left-hand steering	左邊方向盤	「左駕的車」有以下兩種說法： ① a left-hand-drive car ② a car with left-hand drive

有些國家幅員遼闊，因此在交通不方便的地區，出門就得仰賴車子。如果你要去較偏僻的地方觀光，那最好在國內辦好國際駕照和租車手續，這樣到了當地拿車才比較方便。

如果要在當地租車，可以在機場的觀光服務中心、租車櫃檯或是在飯店辦理手續。辦理時需要出示護照、國際駕照和信用卡。另外，為了以防萬一，最好投保保險。

DIALOGUE 2

Booking a Car Rental Online 線上預訂租車

Ⓐ Is it possible to book a car online next time, to save time?

Ⓑ Yes, just visit our website. You can book your car there.

Ⓐ What's the booking process?

Ⓑ Just choose your model and the date and location of your pick-up. We'll have the car ready for you when you arrive.

Ⓐ Is it cheaper to book a car online than in person?

Ⓑ We often have Internet-only deals. So yes, it can be cheaper to rent online.

Ⓐ 為了節省時間，下次我可以線上預訂租車嗎？

Ⓑ 可以的，只要上我們的網站，就可以預訂租車。

Ⓐ 預訂流程是什麼呢？

Ⓑ 只要選擇您要預訂的車種，然後選定您的取車日期和地點。我們就會在您抵達時將車準備好。

Ⓐ 線上預訂租車會比親自來租還便宜嗎？

Ⓑ 我們通常會有線上專屬優惠價，所以線上預訂是有可能比較便宜。

Study Points

book a car	預訂租車	book 當動詞為「預訂」之意，同義詞還有 reserve。
pick-up	取車	在此作名詞使用。
have the car ready	將車準備好	此處的 have 為使役動詞，後接原形動詞或形容詞。
in person	親自	介系詞要用 in。

ONLINE CAR RENTAL
線上租車
示例介面

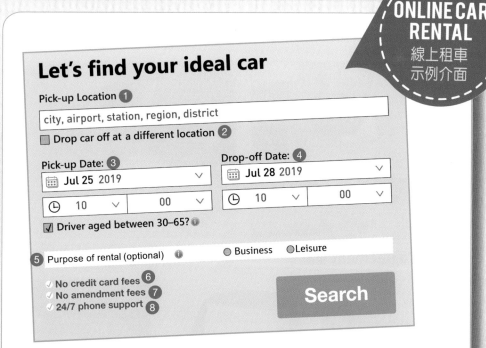

Let's find your ideal car

Pick-up Location ❶

city, airport, station, region, district

☐ **Drop car off at a different location ❷**

Pick-up Date: ❸
🗓 Jul 25 2019 ⌄
🕙 10 ⌄ 00 ⌄

Drop-off Date: ❹
🗓 Jul 28 2019 ⌄
🕙 10 ⌄ 00 ⌄

☑ **Driver aged between 30–65?** ⓘ

❺ Purpose of rental (optional) ⓘ ⚪ Business ⚪ Leisure

✓ **No credit card fees ❻**
✓ **No amendment fees ❼**
✓ **24/7 phone support ❽**

Search

❶ Pick-up Location 取車地點

❷ Drop car off at a different location 甲地租乙地還

❸ Pick-up Date 取車日期

❹ Drop-off Date 還車日期

❺ Purpose of rental (optional) Business/Leisure
租車用途（選填）
出差／出遊

❻ No credit card fees
無信用卡衍生費用

❼ No amendment fees 無改單費用

❽ 24/7 phone support
24小時電話支援

(cc by Tony Webster)

1 **IDP (International Driving Permit)** 國際駕照

2 **car insurance** 汽車險

3 **rental agreement** 租約

4 **rental charge** 租金

5 **deposit** 保證金；押金

6 **no-show fee** 違約金（無故放棄費用）

7 **mileage** 哩程數

8 **gas station** 加油站

9 **gas pump** 油泵

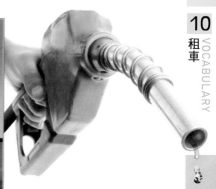
10 **gas pump nozzle** 油槍

11 **regular gasoline** 普通汽油

12 **plus gasoline** 次高級汽油

13 **premium gasoline** 高級汽油

14 **diesel fuel** 柴油

15 **unleaded gasoline** 無鉛汽油

16 **broken down** 拋錨

17 **flat tire** 爆胎

18 **under construction** 道路施工

 **19** **parking lot** 停車場

 **20** **parking space** 停車位

 **21** **parking meter** 停車計費表

 **22** **road map** 交通路線圖

 **23** **traffic sign; road sign** 交通標誌

ROAD SIGNS
路標

STOP
停車再開

DO NOT ENTER
禁止進入

YIELD
讓道

DETOUR
繞道

RAILROAD CROSSING
鐵路平交道

DEAD END
此路不通

ONE WAY
單行道

INTERSTATE ROUTE
州際公路

U.S. ROUTE
美國國道

MINIMUM SPEED
最低速限

SPEED LIMIT
最高速限

DO NOT PASS
禁止通行

NO U-TURN
禁止迴轉

NO LEFT TURN
禁止左轉

NO RIGHT TURN
禁止右轉

NO MOTOR VEHICLES
禁止汽機車通行

Useful Expressions

1 找租車公司

1 Where can I rent a car? 我可以在哪裡租到車子呢？

2 Are there any car rental companies around here?
這附近有租車公司嗎？

3 Where's the nearest rent-a-car company?
最近的租車公司在哪裡？

4 I want to rent a car, but how do I go about it?
我想要租車，我應該如何辦理呢？

2 到租車公司租車

5 I made a reservation in Taiwan. My name is Amy Lee.
我叫李艾美，我在台灣已經預約好了。

6 I have a reservation. My name is Ginny Lin.
我有預租，我叫林金妮。

7 I'd like to rent a car. 我要租輛車。

8 Do you have one available now? 現在有車子可以租用嗎？

9 May I see a price list? 我可以看一下價目表嗎？

10 Can I see your rent-a-car list?
我可以看一下出租車輛的清單嗎？

11 ① What type of a car would you like?
② What model do you want?
您想租哪一種款式的車？

12 What kind of cars do you have? 有哪幾種車款呢？

13 I'd like one that gets good gas mileage.
我想要較省油的車。

14 Do you have Japanese cars? 有日本車嗎？

15 Do you have any sports cars? 有跑車嗎？

16 An automatic sedan, please. 我想要租一輛自排的轎車。

17 I'd like a compact car. 我想要租一輛小型車。

18 I'd like a small van. 我想要租一輛小型箱型車。

19 I'd like an SUV. 我想要租一輛休旅車。〔SUV = sport-utility vehicle〕

Types of Cars 車子種類

sedan car 轎車

van 箱型車

compact car 小型車

SUV 休旅車

limousine 豪華轎車

hybrid car 油電混合車

20 I'd like one with an automatic transmission.
我想要租一輛自排車。

21 I prefer a manual transmission.
我想要租手排車。

manual car
手排車

automatic car
自排車

22 How many days do you want to rent this car?
這輛車你要租幾天？

23 I'd like to rent it for one day. 我想要租一天。

24 I'd like to rent this type of car for a week.
這種車款我想要租一個星期。

25 ① Can I leave it at my destination?
② Can I drop it off at my destination?
可以在我要去的地方還車嗎？

26 I'd like to rent a car for a one-way trip only.
我想租可以在目的地還車的車子。

27 Can I leave the car at any rental office in the country?
我可以在國內的任何營業所還車嗎？

28 What's the drop-off charge? 中途還車的費用是多少？

29 When do I have to return the car? 最遲是什麼時候要還車？

30 Where do I return the car? 我要在哪裡還車？

3 詢問費用及保險

31　① What is the rate?
　　② How much does it cost? 租車費用是多少錢？

32　I'll pay by credit card. 我用信用卡付帳。

33　Is the mileage free? 沒有限制行駛哩數嗎？

34　① Does it include gas?
　　② Is the cost of gas included in that? 有含油費嗎？

35　① Do I have to pay a deposit?
　　② Do you need a deposit? 需要付押金嗎？

36　Does the price include insurance? 這個費用有含保險嗎？

37　Is the insurance charge separate? 保險費另外算嗎？

38　① I'd like to insure it.
　　② I'd like to buy insurance. 我想要買保險。

39　I'd like full insurance. 我想要買全險。

40　Am I fully covered in case of an accident?
　　發生事故時，保險公司會全部給付嗎？

41　What's the extra charge if I don't return it on time?
　　如果車子沒有準時歸還的話，那逾期的費用要怎麼算呢？

42　How much will it be if I go over the rental period?
　　如果超過歸還日期，要加付多少錢呢？

43 Is there a gas station around here? 這附近有加油站嗎？

44 My car is out of gas. 我的車沒油了。

45 Fill it up, please. 請加滿。

46 Fill it up with regular, please. 普通汽油，請加滿。

47 Ten dollars of gas, please. 麻煩加十塊美金的汽油。

48 Five gallons of gas, please. 麻煩加五加侖的汽油。

49 How much is it per gallon? 一加侖的汽油是多少錢？

50 Please show me how to fill the gas tank. 請教我怎麼加油。

51 How do I use this pump? 這個油槍要怎麼使用呢？

52 Check the battery, please. 請幫我檢查電瓶。

53 Charge the battery, please. 請幫我把電瓶充電。

54 Check the brakes, please. 請幫我檢查煞車。

55 Check the tires, please. 請幫我檢查輪胎。

56 Wash the car, please. 請幫我洗車。

57 Clean the windshield, please. 請幫我清洗擋風玻璃。

58 My car has broken down. 我的車故障了。

59 This car isn't in good condition. 這輛車的狀況不太好。

60 It makes a strange noise. 它會發出奇怪的聲音。

61 I've got a flat. 我的車爆胎了。

62 The engine won't start. 引擎無法發動。

如果要租車，建議在出發前先上網或是打電話訂車，車商就會在約定的時間，將車子送到指定地點或機場。

需特別注意，在英、紐澳等國開車是右座駕駛（right-hand drive），不同於國內的左駕（left-hand drive），開車時要特別小心。租車前建議先試車，並檢查車子本身是否有刮痕或受損，這些都須在事前先跟車行人員說清楚。若真的發生事故，該由哪一方承擔責任，也都必須先當面談清，以免事後衍生更多問題。

國際駕照（International Driving Permit）申辦

(cc by Ywang.tw)

若要出國自駕，務必要在出國前先辦好國際駕照，申辦方式如下：

★ 換國際駕照所需證件：
　① 身分證或居留證正本
　　（若為代委託辦理，則請代辦人攜帶雙證件）
　② 原駕照正本
　③ 2 吋半身照片 2 張
　④ 護照影本（用以查核英文姓名及出生地）

★ 申辦費用：250 元

★ 申辦地點：監理站的「駕照綜合窗口」

CAR PARTS
汽車構造

windshield 擋風玻璃

side/wing mirror 後照鏡

windshield wiper 雨刷

trunk 後行李箱

hood 車蓋

headlight 車燈

tire 輪胎

signal light 方向燈

license plate 車牌

bumper 保險桿

steering wheel 方向盤

emergency brake 手煞車

gauge 儀表

dashboard 儀錶板

horn 喇叭

gear 排檔桿

driver's seat 駕駛座

passenger seat 副駕駛座

back seat 後座

child safety seat
兒童安全座椅

rear-view mirror 後視鏡

**GPS (global positioning
system)** 導航系統

exhaust pipe 排氣管

engine 引擎

battery 電瓶

jumper cables 救車線

**emergency warning
triangle** 三角警示牌

traffic cone 交通錐

11 問路

ASKING FOR DIRECTIONS

DIALOGUE 1

Finding the Way 問路  086

Ⓐ Excuse me. Can you tell me the way to the Hilton Hotel?

Ⓑ Go straight down this street about five blocks, and you'll see a drugstore on the corner. When you get there, turn right. You'll see it just on your left.

Ⓐ How long will it take me to get there on foot?

Ⓑ About 7 minutes.

Ⓐ I see. Thanks for your help.

Ⓐ 不好意思,請問希爾頓飯店要怎麼走?

Ⓑ 這條馬路直走大約五條街左右,轉角處有間藥房,看到藥房後右轉,右轉後的左手邊就可以看到了。

Ⓐ 從這裡走過去要多久?

Ⓑ 大概7分鐘左右。

Ⓐ 哦,那我知道了,謝謝你。

Study Points

Can you tell me the way to . . . ?	請問去……要怎麼走？	較客氣的問路説法
Go straight down . . .	往……一直走	在美國，道路的單位都是用 block
turn right	右轉	也可以説成：turn to the right
just on your left	就在你的左手邊	介系詞要用 on
Thanks for your help.	謝謝您的幫助。	記得要禮貌地感謝對方

若在國外迷了路，請不要害怕，鼓起勇氣向陌生人問個路吧！
問路時，可以這麼説：

- **Excuse me. Can you tell me how to get to . . . ?**
  不好意思，請問一下，
  到……要怎麼走呢？

- **Excuse me. Do you know where the . . . is ?**
  不好意思，請問一下，
  ……在哪裡呢？

1 **lose one's way** 迷路

2 **landmark** 地標

3 **direction** 方向

4 **block** 街區

5 **cross the street** 穿越馬路

6 **pass the station** 路過車站

7 at the intersection 在十字路口

8 at the corner 在轉角

9 on your left 在你的左手邊

10 on your right 在你的右手邊

11 turn left 左轉　**12 turn right** 右轉

13 go straight 直走

Useful Expressions

❶ Excuse me. I think I've lost my way. Where am I now?
不好意思，我迷路了。請問這裡是哪裡？

❷ I'm a stranger here. 我對這裡不熟。

❸ I'm not familiar with this area. 這附近我不熟。

❹ Where am I now on this map?
我現在在這張地圖上的哪個位置？

❺ Please show me where I am on this map.
可以請你指給我看我現在在地圖上的哪個地方嗎？

❻ Where does this street lead to? 這條路通往哪裡？

❼ What's the name of this street? 這條街的街名是什麼？

❽ What street is this? 這是哪一條街？

❾ Which way is north? 哪邊是北邊？

❿ What part of the city is this? 這裡是位於市區的哪一邊？

⓫ Do you have any idea where this address is?
你知道這個住址在哪裡嗎？

⓬ How do I get to this address [place]?
要怎麼去這個住址〔地方〕呢？

2 詢問路線

⑬ Where is the bus stop, please?
請問公車站在哪裡呢？

⑭ Where is the nearest station?
最近的車站在哪裡？

⑮ Can you show me the way to the nearest subway station?
請問最近的地鐵站要怎麼走呢？

⑯ How do I get to Hyde Park? 請問去海德公園要怎麼走？

⑰ Can you tell me how to get to the zoo?
請問動物園要怎麼去？

⑱ Do you know the way to the Hilton Hotel?
請問去希爾頓飯店要怎麼走？

⑲ Where is the Central Bank? 中央銀行在哪裡呢？

⑳ Is this the right way to the British Museum?
去大英博物館走這條路對嗎？

㉑ What's the shortcut to Plaza Hollywood?
去好萊塢廣場的捷徑是什麼？

㉒ On which side of the street? 在馬路的哪一邊呢？

㉓ Is it correct to go straight? 一直直走就是了嗎？

㉔ Are there any landmarks along the way?
沿路上有什麼明顯地標嗎？

25
1. You won't miss it.
2. You can't miss it. 那很好找的。

26
- **A** How long will it take on foot?
- **B** It's about a 10-minute walk from here.
- **A** 走路的話，要走多久？
- **B** 從這裡大概要走十分鐘的路程。

27
- **A** How far is it from here?
- **B** About 500 meters.
- **A** 離這裡有多遠的距離？
- **B** 大概五百公尺。

28
- **A** Is it (very) far from here?
- **B** No, it's not that far.
- **A** 離這裡（很）遠嗎？
- **B** 不會啦，不會太遠。

29
1. Can I walk there?
2. Can I get there on foot? 走路可以到嗎？

30
1. You should take a bus.
2. You should go by bus. 你還是搭公車去比較好。

31 Which direction is 42nd Street? 第42條街是哪個方向？

W.C. (原指 water closet，比較少用)

3　詢問洗手間

32　Excuse me. Where can I find a restroom?
請問洗手間在哪裡？

33　Excuse me. Do you have a restroom? 請問有洗手間嗎？

34　Is there a restroom nearby? 這附近有洗手間嗎？

35　Where is the restroom? 哪裡有洗手間呢？

36　Where is the nearest restroom? 最近的洗手間在哪裡呢？

37　May I use your restroom? 可以借個洗手間嗎？

38　Where's the men's room? 男廁在哪裡？

39　Where's the ladies' room? 女廁在哪裡？

40　It is occupied. 有人在用。

41　It is vacant. 沒有人在用。

RECEIVED

12 觀光
SIGHTSEEING

DIALOGUE 1
Sightseeing Tours 觀光行程 `091`

Ⓐ Do you have any sightseeing tours of the city?

Ⓑ We have half-day tours, full-day tours, and nighttime tours available.

Ⓐ Which tour includes more famous places?

Ⓑ You'd probably like the full-day tour the best. Niagara Falls is included in the itinerary.

Ⓐ Does the tour include a guide?

Ⓑ Yes, we have a Chinese-speaking guide.

Ⓐ 有沒有市區的觀光行程？

Ⓑ 有半日遊、一日遊和夜間觀光等行程。

Ⓐ 哪個團的知名景點比較多？

Ⓑ 那你可能會比較喜歡一日遊，這個行程有包含去尼加拉瓜大瀑布。

Ⓐ 那個行程會有導遊跟著嗎？

Ⓑ 有的，有會說中文的導遊。

Study Points

sightseeing tour	觀光團	sightseer 是「觀光客」
half-day tours, full-day tours, and nighttime tours	半日遊、一日遊和夜間行程	nighttime 是「夜間的」
available	可得到的	available 的發音是 [əˋveləbl̩]
itinerary	旅遊行程	itinerary 的發音是 [aɪˋtɪnəˌrɛrɪ]
a tour includes a guide	含導遊同行的行程	guide 是「導遊」

雖然在出國觀光之前，可以從許多的網路、情報雜誌或觀光旅遊的書籍中獲取許多資訊，但實際去參觀的時候可能多少會有落差。

這時候你可以去當地的**遊客中心**（tourist information），索取最新情報。想要有不一樣的玩法，只要好好地利用旅客服務中心，就可以挖到很多寶貴的資料喔。

1 **travel agency** 旅行社

2 **tourist information** 遊客中心

3 **tourist** 遊客

4 **tour group** 旅遊團

5 **tour guide** 導遊

6 **sightseeing bus** 觀光巴士

7 **itinerary** 旅遊行程

8 **guidebook** 旅遊指南

9 **spot** 景點

10 **gift shop** 禮品店

11 **take pictures** 拍照

12 **photograph** 相片

Useful Expressions

❶ Can you tell me where the tourist information office is?
請問旅客服務中心在哪裡？

❷ Do you have a city map? 這裡有市區地圖嗎？

❸ Do you have a free map of this area?
有沒有可以免費索取的當地地圖呢？

❹ I'd like a bus route map. 我想要一張公車路線圖。

❺ Where can I get a New York Subway map?
在哪裡可以拿到紐約地鐵的路線圖呢？

❻ Are there any tour guidebooks? 有沒有觀光的旅遊指南呢？

❼ Do you have a brochure for sightseeing?
有觀光手冊嗎？

2 詢問觀光行程

8 I'd like to see the sights of the city. 我想要做市區觀光。

9 Do you have any sightseeing tours of the city?
有市區觀光團嗎？

10 I'd like to take a sightseeing tour. 我想報名參加觀光團。

11 What kind of tours do you have? 有哪些行程呢？

12 Can you recommend some popular tours?
可以推薦一些比較受歡迎的行程給我嗎？

13 Do you have a full-day tour?
有沒有一日遊的團呢？

14 What kind of sightseeing bus tours do you have?
有哪些觀光巴士的團呢？

15 Do you have any half-day sightseeing bus tours?
有沒有半天的觀光巴士團呢？

16 I'd like to sign up for the Niagara Falls tour.
我想報名參加尼加拉瓜大瀑布的旅遊團。

17 Which tour is best for seeing museums?
要參觀博物館的話，選哪個行程最好？

18 Is there a tour that includes a Broadway show?
有沒有可以看百老匯的團呢？

19 Do you have any tours of the islands? 有環島的旅行團嗎？

3 詢問旅遊團細節

20 Would you please give me some details about the tour?
可以告訴我這個行程的一些詳細內容嗎？

21 Is it a half-day tour? 那是半天的行程嗎？

22 What can I see on the tour? 那個團是參觀什麼的呢？

23 Does it include a visit to Disneyland?
那個團有去迪士尼樂園嗎？

24 How long is the tour? 這個團會去多久？

25 Is lunch included in the tour? 這個團有包含午餐嗎？

26 What is the charge? 費用是多少呢？

27 Does the charge include meals? 有含伙食費嗎？

28 I'd prefer something less expensive than this tour.
我想找比這個更便宜的團。

29 What is the difference between this tour and the more expensive ones? 這個團跟那個比較貴的團，有什麼不一樣呢？

30 Where will we have lunch? 中午是在哪裡用餐呢？

31 Where do we get on the bus? 在哪裡搭巴士呢？

32 What time does the tour start? 幾點出發呢？

33 When and from where does it leave? 幾點在哪裡出發呢？

34 What time and where should we wait?
我們應該幾點在哪裡等呢？

35 Will we have any free time during the tour?
在行程中有自由時間嗎？

36 Do you have a Chinese-speaking guide?
有會說中文的導遊一起去嗎？

37 Does the guide speak any languages other than English?
導遊會說英文以外的其他語言嗎？

TOURIST SIGNS
觀光景點指標

Ticket Sales
售票處

Historic Building
古蹟建築

Cinema
電影院

Café
咖啡廳

Museum
博物館

Photography
照相服務

Beach
海灘

Restaurant
餐廳

4 觀光景點 🎧096

38 What time does this museum open?
這間博物館是幾點開門？

39 How much is the admission fee? 門票是多少錢？

40 Two adults and three children, please.
麻煩給我兩張全票和三張兒童票。

41 One student ticket, please. 請給我一張學生票。

42 Can I take pictures inside the museum?
博物館裡面可以照相嗎？

43 May I take a picture of this building?
我可以拍這棟建築物嗎？

44 Is this the correct way? 往這邊走沒錯吧？

45 Where is the entrance? 入口在哪裡？

46 What's that structure [building]? 那棟建築物是什麼？

47 Can I go into this building? 可以進去這棟建築物裡面嗎？

48 When was it built? 它是什麼時候建造的？

49 How old is it? 它有多久歷史了？

50 What's it famous for? 它是以什麼聞名的呢？

51 Where is the gift shop? 哪裡有禮品店呢？

52 What time shall we meet next? 下次的集合時間是什麼時候？

53 What time should I be back? 在幾點之前一定要回來集合呢？

5 拍照 (097)

54 May I take pictures here? 這裡可以拍照嗎？

55 Would you take a picture for me? 可以請你幫我照張相嗎？

56 Can you please take a picture for us?
不好意思，可以請你幫我們拍照嗎？

57 Just press this button. 只要按下這個鈕就行了。

58 Take a picture with that building in the background,
please. 請以那棟建築物為背景，幫我們拍照。

59 Please push the button after the red light comes on.
請等紅色的燈亮了之後，再按鈕。

60 One more, please. 麻煩再照一張。

61 Excuse me. May I take your picture, please?
不好意思，可以讓我拍您嗎？

62 Excuse me. Could I please take a picture with you?
不好意思，我可以跟您一起照張相嗎？

63 Would you pose with me? 您可以跟我合照嗎？

13 生病
SICKNESS

I Have a Slight Fever 我有點發燒 （098）

A What's the matter?

B I have a slight fever, and I also have pain on the right side of my chest when I cough.

A Where does it hurt?

B Right in this area. I am having difficulty breathing.

A Let's check your chest. Take a deep breath. Let it out slowly. How do you feel now?

B I feel better now.

A OK, there is nothing to worry about. Maybe it was caused by fatigue from the long journey.

A 你怎麼了？

B 我有點發燒，而且只要一咳嗽，右邊的胸口就會疼痛。

A 是哪裡痛？

B 這邊，然後會覺得呼吸困難。

A 那我來檢查一下你的胸部。深呼吸，把氣慢慢地吐出來。你現在覺得怎麼樣？

B 我覺得好多了。

A 這大概是長程旅行所引起的疲勞，不用擔心。

I have a . . .	我有……（症狀）	跟醫生說明自己症狀時的表達方式
have difficulty breathing	呼吸困難	「have difficulty . . .」表示對某事有困難
take a deep breath	深呼吸	動詞要用 take
feel better	感覺好些	用來表達身體感覺好一點
nothing to worry about	不用擔心	用來表達身體沒有大礙

出外旅行時，為了預防在國外生病，盡可能不要飲用生水，或是玩得過頭。萬一不小心生病了，也是要去看醫生喔！

歐美貫徹醫藥分級制度，所以除了阿斯匹靈、止瀉藥和一般外傷的藥之外，如果沒有醫師的處方箋，無法輕易在藥局買到其他的藥物。而且，歐美的醫療機構大都是採預約制，所以生病時要先用電話預約看病，如果情況很危急，可以到大醫院的急診處就醫。

在美國，警察、消防隊和救護車的緊急電話號碼都是911。接通救護車的電話時，可以說：

■ **Ambulance, please.**
我要叫救護車。

ambulance 救護車

fire truck 消防車

tow truck 拖吊車

police car 警車

1 hospital 綜合醫院

2 clinic 診所

3 pharmacy; drugstore 藥房

4 first-aid kit 急救箱

5 symptom 症狀

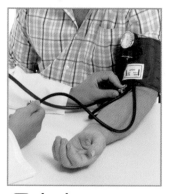

6 checkup 檢查

7 prescription 處方箋

8 injection 打針

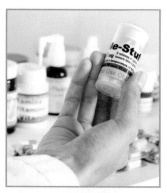

9 medicine 藥

10 **flu** 流行性感冒

11 **cold** 感冒

12 **indigestion** 消化不良

13 **stomachache** 胃痛

14 **food poisoning** 食物中毒

15 **toothache** 牙齒痛

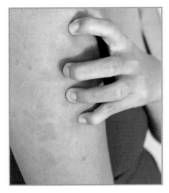

16 **allergy** 過敏

17 **Band-Aid** OK繃

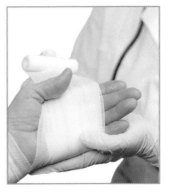

18 **trauma** 外傷

DIFFERENT KINDS OF PAIN
疼痛種類

1	acute pain	急性疼痛
2	sudden pain	突然痛起來
3	chronic pain	慢性疼痛
4	sharp pain	刺痛
5	dull pain	隱隱作痛
6	severe pain	極度疼痛
7	stinging pain	刺痛
8	throbbing pain	抽痛
9	gripping pain	絞痛
10	splitting pain	割傷的痛
11	continuous pain	連續不斷的痛

DISEASE
疾病名稱

1	high blood pressure	高血壓
2	diabetes	糖尿病
3	heart disease	心臟病
4	heart attack	心臟病發
5	asthma	氣喘
6	cancer	癌症
7	gout	痛風
8	depression	憂鬱症

HOSPITAL UNITS
醫院單位

Registration Office	掛號處
Emergency Room	急診室
First Aid Station	急救站
Appointments	預約門診
Waiting Room	候診室
Consultation Room	診療室
Medication and Injection	吃藥及注射室
Cashier	批價處
Dispensary	領藥處
Pharmacy	藥局
Diagnosis Certificates	診斷證明書
Outpatient Department	門診部
Inpatient Department	住院部
Admission Information	住院服務中心
Discharge	出院處
Intensive Care Unit	加護病房
Ward	病房
Operation Room (OR)	手術室
Family Lounge	家屬休息室
Patient Beds Only	病床專用電梯
Mortuary	太平間

Medical Department	內科
Surgical Department	外科
Pediatrics Department	小兒科
Obstetrics and Gynecology Department	婦產科
Ophthalmology Department	眼科
Dental Department	牙科
ENT (Ear-Nose-Throat) Department	耳鼻喉科
Urology Department	泌尿科
Dermatology Department	皮膚科
Orthopedic Surgery Department	矯形外科
Trauma Department	創傷外科
Plastic Surgery	整形外科
Cardiology Department	心臟病科
Psychiatry Department	精神病科
Orthopedics Department	骨科
Neurology Department	神經科

HUMAN BODY
人體部位

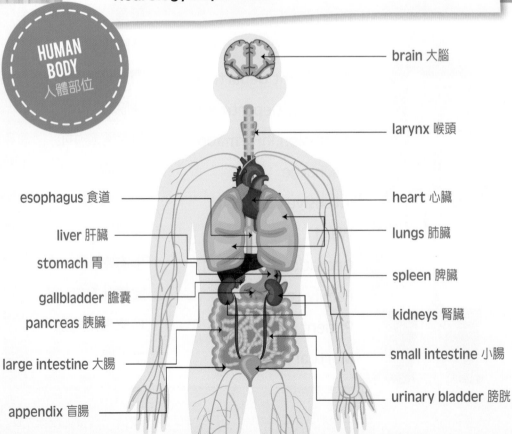

brain 大腦

larynx 喉頭

esophagus 食道

heart 心臟

liver 肝臟

lungs 肺臟

stomach 胃

gallbladder 膽囊

spleen 脾臟

pancreas 胰臟

kidneys 腎臟

large intestine 大腸

small intestine 小腸

appendix 盲腸

urinary bladder 膀胱

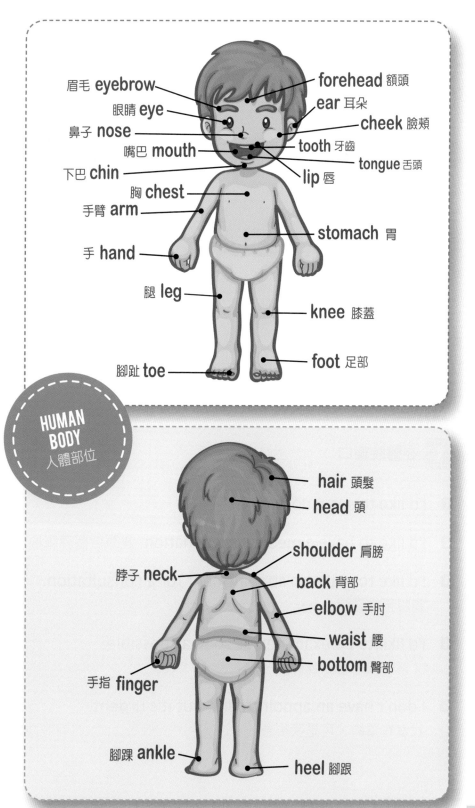

眉毛 eyebrow
眼睛 eye
鼻子 nose
嘴巴 mouth
下巴 chin
胸 chest
手臂 arm
手 hand
腿 leg
腳趾 toe

forehead 額頭
ear 耳朵
cheek 臉頰
tooth 牙齒
tongue 舌頭
lip 唇
stomach 胃
knee 膝蓋
foot 足部

HUMAN BODY
人體部位

hair 頭髮
head 頭
shoulder 肩膀
脖子 neck
back 背部
elbow 手肘
waist 腰
bottom 臀部
手指 finger
腳踝 ankle
heel 腳跟

Useful Expressions

make an appointment
預約看診

take one's temperature
量體溫

take one's blood pressure
量血壓

1 在醫院窗口

❶ I'd like to see a doctor. 我想要看病。

❷ I'd like to have a medical examination. 我想做個健康檢查。

❸ I'd like to make an appointment for a consultation.
我想預約看病。

❹ I'd like to be examined as soon as possible.
（沒有預約時）我想快一點看診。

❺ I don't have an appointment, but it's urgent.
我沒有預約，可是我很急。

COMMON COLD SYMPTOMS
常見的
感冒症狀

fever 發燒

headache 頭痛

sore throat 喉嚨痛

cough 咳嗽

runny nose 流鼻水

stuffy nose 鼻塞

sneeze 打噴嚏

2 身體症狀

6 I have a slight fever. 我有點發燒。

7 I feel feverish. 我可能發燒了。

8 I have a 39.5 degree Centigrade fever.
我燒到攝氏39.5度。

9 My temperature rose suddenly. 我突然發高燒。

10 I've had a high temperature for some time now.
我一直高燒不退。

11 I feel chilly. 我覺得全身發冷。

12 I'm afraid I've caught a cold. 我好像感冒了。

13 ① I have a slight cold.
② I've caught a bit of a cold. 我得了輕微的感冒。

14 I've got a head cold. 我鼻塞感冒。

15 I can't get rid of this cold. 我感冒一直沒有好。

16 I feel languid. 我覺得渾身無力。

17 I feel dizzy when I stand up. 我站起來就覺得頭昏眼花。

18 I don't feel well. 我不太舒服。

19 I feel very sick. 我覺得很不舒服。

20 I cannot sleep. 我睡不著。

21 I feel dizzy. 我覺得頭暈。

22 ① I feel like vomiting.
② I feel like throwing up. 我想吐。

23 I vomited last night. 我昨晚吐了。

24 I can't keep any food down. 我不管吃什麼都會吐。

25 ① I don't have an appetite.
② I don't feel like eating. 我沒有食欲。

26 I have high blood pressure. 我有高血壓。

27 I can't stop sneezing. 我一直打噴嚏。

28 I can't stop coughing. 我一直咳嗽。

3 頭、脖子等症狀

㉙ I have a headache. 我頭痛。

㉚ My head is throbbing. 我覺得頭陣陣抽痛。

㉛ I have a splitting headache. 我覺得頭痛得要裂開了。

㉜ I feel heavy in the head. 我覺得頭暈。

㉝ I have a migraine. 我有偏頭痛。

㉞ I have a crick in my neck. 我脖子痙攣。

㉟ I strained my neck. 我的脖子扭到了。

4 嘴、喉嚨、牙齒等症狀 103

㊱ My mouth is rough. 我的嘴巴破了。

㊲ I have inflammation in my mouth. 我的嘴巴發炎了。

㊳ My mouth is swollen. 我的嘴巴腫起來。

㊴ I have a sore throat. 我喉嚨痛。

㊵ I have swollen tonsils. 我扁桃腺發炎。

㊶ I have a toothache. 我牙痛。

㊷ My teeth feel unduly sensitive. 我的牙齒對冷熱很敏感。

㊸ My decayed tooth aches. 我的蛀牙在痛。

5 鼻、眼、耳等症狀

44 There is swelling in my nose. 我鼻子裡面腫起來了。

45 I have a stuffed nose. 我鼻塞。

46 My nose is runny. 我流鼻水。

47 My eyes hurt. 我眼睛痛。

48 My right eye is swollen. 我右邊的眼睛腫起來了。

49 There is a ringing in my ears. 我覺得耳鳴。

50 I have a severe earache. 我耳朵很痛。

6 胸部和腹部的症狀 (105)

51 I have heart trouble. 我有心臟病的問題。

52 I suffer from asthma. 我有氣喘。

53 My chest hurts. 我覺得胸口難受。

54 I've got a pain in my chest. 我胸口痛。

55 I feel choked up. 我覺得呼吸困難。

56 My chest hurts when I breathe. 我一呼吸，胸口就會痛。

57 I have a stomachache. 我胃痛。

58 I have abdominal pain on my left side. 我左側腹痛。

59 My stomach burns. 我胃在灼痛。

60 I have heartburn. 我覺得胃灼熱。

61 My stomach aches after I eat a meal. 我吃完飯後胃就在痛。

62 I have a gripping pain in my stomach. 我胃絞痛。

63 I feel as if I have a bulging, stuffed stomach. 我覺得胃很脹。

64 I have a heavy stomach. 我胃消化不良。

65 I have an upset stomach. 我拉肚子。

66 I have loose bowels. 我拉肚子。

67 I have had no bowel movement for three days.
我有三天沒排便了。

68 I suffer from constipation. 我有便秘。

69 I have terrible menstrual pain. 我生理痛，痛得很厲害。

vomit 嘔吐　　fart 放屁　　diarrhea 拉肚子　　constipation 便秘

7 背部、腰、肩、關節等症狀

70 ① I have a pain in my back.
② I have a backache. 我的背會痛。

71 I suffer from terrible back pain. 我的背痛得很厲害。

72 My joints ache. 我關節痛。

73 I've strained my back. 我的背閃到了。

74 I often have cramps when sleeping.
我睡覺的時候常會抽筋。

75 I have terribly stiff shoulders. 我的肩膀很僵硬。

8 過敏與外傷 107

76 I have severe hives. 我的蕁麻疹很嚴重。

77 I feel itchy all over my body. 我覺得全身發癢。

78 I'm allergic to antibiotics. 我對抗生素過敏。

79 I'm injured. 我受傷了。

80 I'm badly hurt. 我傷得很嚴重。

81 I've broken my leg. 我摔斷腿了。

82 I think I twisted my foot. 我的腳好像扭傷了。

83 My shoulder is badly bruised. 我肩膀擦傷得很嚴重。

swelling 腫脹　　bruise 青腫　　fracture 骨折

sprain
扭傷

bleeding
流血

---

84 I'm afraid I've dislocated my left arm.
我的左手好像脫臼了。

---

85 I burned my finger. 我的手指燙傷了。

---

86 It's bleeding. 流血了。

---

9 醫生對病患說的話

87 ① Is something bothering you?
② What seems to be the trouble? 你哪裡不舒服嗎？

---

88 What kind of pain are you having? 怎麼個痛法？

physician 內科醫生

surgeon 外科醫生

dentist 牙醫

89 **How long have you had this pain?** 你從什麼時候開始痛的？

90 **Point to where it hurts.** 請用手指指給我看你哪邊痛。

91 **Do you have an appetite?** 你食欲好嗎？

92 **What did you eat yesterday?** 你昨天吃了什麼東西？

93 **Do you have diarrhea?** 你有拉肚子嗎？

94 **Did you have a bowel movement this morning?**
你今天早上有排便嗎？

95 **Have you been sleeping well?** 你最近睡得好嗎？

96 **Let's take a look.** 讓我來檢查看看。

97 **Let's take your temperature.** 量一下你的體溫。

98 **Let's take your blood pressure.** 量一下你的血壓。

99 **Let's take your pulse.** 量一下你的脈搏。

100 **I want you to have an X-ray.** 你要去照張X光。

ALLERGY SYMPTOMS
過敏症狀

RASH
紅疹

LACRIMATION
流淚

RUNNY NOSE
流鼻水

SNEEZING
打噴嚏

101 Do you have any allergies? 你會過敏嗎？

102 Do you have any other medical conditions?
你有什麼其他疾病嗎？

103 Roll up your sleeve. 把你的袖子捲起來。

104 Take off your shirt, please. 請把你的襯衫脫下來。

105 Unbutton your shirt, please. 請解開襯衫的鈕扣。

106 Open your mouth wide and say "Ah."
把你的嘴巴張大一點，說聲「啊」。

107 Take a deep breath. 深呼吸。

108 Lie down here. 躺在這裡。

109 Breathe out . . . in . . . 吐氣⋯⋯，吸氣⋯⋯。

110 Breathe in slowly. 慢慢吸氣。

111 You shouldn't eat greasy foods. 你要避免吃太油的食物。

112 You shouldn't drink too much alcohol.
你要避免喝太多含有酒精的飲料。

113 You shouldn't drink any alcohol.
你不可以喝任何含酒精的飲料。

114 Please stop smoking and drinking. 不可以吸菸或喝酒。

115 Please see a doctor tomorrow. 請明天再來複診。

116 Please see a doctor if the symptom worsens.
如果症狀變嚴重了，你就要再去看醫生。

117 I'll write a prescription for you. 我會開藥方給你。

118 I'll give you a prescription, and you can have it filled at a drugstore. 我會開處方箋給你，請拿到藥局配藥。

119 Take this prescription to a pharmacy. You can get the medicine there. 請拿著這張處方箋到藥局拿藥。

10 到藥局買藥

120 Is there a pharmacy nearby? 這附近有藥局嗎？

121 Here is my prescription. 這是我的處方箋。

122 Can I get my prescription filled here?
這裡可以配藥嗎？

123 Please fill this prescription. 請幫我配這張處方箋的藥。

124 Would you fill this prescription, please?
請照這張處方箋配藥。

125
Ⓐ Do I need a prescription to buy this?
Ⓑ These tablets are available over-the-counter.
Ⓐ 要有處方箋才可以買到這個藥嗎？
Ⓑ 這些藥片沒有處方箋也可以買。

126 I need some medicine. 請給我一些藥。

127 Do you have stomach medicine? 有胃藥嗎？

128 I need something to help me sleep.
我需要一些可以幫助睡眠的藥。

129 I want medicine for a cold. 我需要感冒藥。

130 ① Does it have any side effects?
② Are there any side effects? 這個藥有副作用嗎？

131 How many of these tablets should I take?
我要吃幾個藥片呢？

132 When do I take them? 藥什麼時候服用呢？

133 How do I take this? 要如何服用呢？

134 Please take it when you feel severe pain.
只有在很痛的時候才要服用。

135 Please take it if the symptoms get worse.
只有症狀嚴重的時候才要服用。

136 Please take it three times a day, after every meal.
一天三次，餐後服用。

137 Please take it twice a day, in the morning and evening.
一天兩次，早、晚服用。

138 Please take it once a day, before you go to bed.
一天一次，睡前服用。

tablet 藥錠

14 失竊或事故
ENCOUNTERING PROBLEMS

DIALOGUE 1
Losing Items 遺失物品 (110)

A I left my bag on the train.

B Which train was it?

A It was the train that just left. I was in a car toward the front of the train.

B What kind of bag is it?

A A small brown bag. It's made of leather.

B What do you have in it?

A My wallet, passport, traveler's checks, and personal effects.

A 我的皮包放在火車上，忘記拿了。

B 是哪一班車呢？

A 就是剛開走的那班車，我剛剛坐在那班車的前面車廂裡。

B 是什麼樣的皮包？

A 是咖啡色的真皮皮包。

B 裡面有什麼東西？

A 有我的錢包、護照、旅行支票，和一些私人物品。

Study Points

It was the train that just left.	就在剛開走的列車上。	just left 指剛剛發班的火車。
a car toward the front of the train	前面的車廂	某節車廂的説法是：I was in the third car from the front (/back). 我在前面（／後面）的第三節車廂。
It's made of . . .	是……材質的	「be made of . . .」指「由……製造而成」，沒有化學或本質改變，如：樹→木桌；be made from 指完全改變原料本質，如：樹→紙。

在海外旅遊，可能會遇到搶劫、遺失護照或貴重物品，或是遇到交通事故等情況，所以要如何預防，或是遇到問題時該怎麼處理，這些都是重要的課題。

最常發生的情況是遇到扒手，所以出門時，最好不要帶太多錢，並且隨時留意自己身邊的東西，尤其是在國外，如果花錢時表現出很有錢的樣子，就很容易為歹徒所覬覦。

所以，為了怕發生搶劫、車禍或是生病，出國前最好先投保海外旅遊平安險（Travel insurance）。

1 lost and found
行李遺失招領處

2 police station 警察局

3 police car 警車

4 policeman 員警

5 embassy 大使館

6 consulate 領事館

7 lost item report
遺失證明

8 theft report
失竊證明

9 missing items
report 遺失證明

I'd like to report the theft as follows. Please make the certificate of the theft.

VICTIM		
FAMILY NAME		
DATE OF BIRTH	GIVEN NANE	
NATIONALITY	DAY / MONTH / YEAR	/
ADDRESS		
ADDRESS IN THIS COUNTRY		
DATE OF THEFT		
DATE / MONTH /	YEAR /	AM. / PM. /
PLACE OF THEFT		
☐ ON THE STREET		
☐ IN THE SUBWAY	☐ AT THE STATION	
☐ IN THE TAXI	☐ IN THE TRAIN/BUS	
☐ AT THE HOTEL ☐ IN THE LOBBY	☐ AT THE AIRPORT	
☐ AT THE SHOP	☐ IN THE ROOM ☐ OTHER	
☐ AT THE MUSEUM	☐ AT RESTAURANT/BAR	
TYPES OF THEFT	☐ OTHER PLACE:	

🔟 **reissue** 重新申請

11 **traffic accident** 交通事故

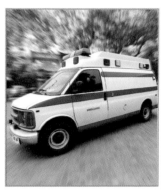

12 **ambulance** 救護車

13 **witness** 目擊證人

14 **damage** 損傷

15 **injured person** 傷患

16 **driver's license** 駕照

17 **license number** 牌照號碼

18 **speed limit** 限速

1 遺失東西 (112)

1 I've lost my wallet. 我的錢包掉了。

2 My wallet is missing. 我的錢包不見了。

3 I dropped my purse somewhere. 我的錢包不知掉在哪裡了。

4 I think I left my wallet in your shop.
我的錢包好像放在你們的店裡，忘記拿走了。

5 It's a red leather wallet. 它是個紅色的皮包。

6 I'm not sure where I left it. 我不太確定它掉到哪裡去了。

7 I left my bag in the taxi. 我把包包留在計程車上忘記拿了。

8 Do you remember the name of the taxi company?
你知道是哪家公司的計程車嗎？

9 I left my briefcase on the train. 我把公事包遺留在火車上了。

10 Have you seen a bag about this size?
你有沒有看到大約這個大小的皮包呢？

wallet 皮夾

purse 錢包

fanny pack 霹靂包

handbag 手提包

briefcase 公事包

suitcase 皮箱

sports bag 運動包

backpack 後背包

luggage 行李箱

2 失竊時

11 My wallet was stolen. 我的錢包被偷了。

12 I lost my wallet with my credit card.
我放有信用卡的錢包被偷了。

13 Somebody picked my pocket. 我的東西被扒走了。

14 I had my wallet stolen from my pocket on the train.
我的錢包在火車上被扒了。

15 A man snatched my bag on the street.
我的包包在街上被一個男人搶走了。

16 My camera was stolen while I was away from my room.
我離開房間後,我的照相機就被偷了。

17 Would you call the police right now?
你可以馬上幫我叫警察嗎?

18
  Ⓐ Hello. Front desk. May I help you?

  Ⓑ I think someone broke into my room.

  Ⓐ 您好,這裡是櫃檯,可以為您效勞嗎?

  Ⓑ 我的房間好像有人闖進來。

19
  Ⓐ What was taken from your room?

  Ⓑ A ring and a watch.

  Ⓐ 您遺失了什麼東西?

  Ⓑ 一只戒指和一支手錶。

3 申報遺失 🎧114

⑳ Where is the lost and found? 失物招領中心在哪裡？

㉑ Where is the nearest police station? 最近的警察局在哪裡？

㉒ Please fill out a missing items report. 請填寫這張遺失清單。

㉓ I'd like to report a theft. 我想要報失竊案。

㉔ I'd like to report a stolen wallet. 我的皮包被偷了，要報案。

㉕ Could you fill out a theft report form?
可以請你開失竊證明書給我嗎？

㉖
Ⓐ What was stolen?
Ⓑ I was robbed of my handbag in front of the hotel near here.
Ⓐ 什麼東西被偷了？
Ⓑ 在這附近的飯店前面，我的手提包被搶了。

㉗
Ⓐ What kind of a handbag is it?
Ⓑ It's a black leather handbag.
Ⓐ 是什麼樣的手提包？
Ⓑ 是一個黑色的皮製手提包。

㉘
Ⓐ What did you have in it?
Ⓑ Passport, traveler's checks, and some cash.
Ⓐ 你的皮包裡有什麼？
Ⓑ 裡面有我的護照、旅行支票，還有一點現金。

29

   Ⓐ How much money were you carrying?

   Ⓑ One hundred dollars in cash, 300 dollars in traveler's checks, and my credit card.

   Ⓐ 裡面有多少錢？

   Ⓑ 有現金100塊和300塊旅行支票，還有信用卡。

30 I had my wallet taken from my pocket. 我的錢包被扒走了。

31 Could you fill out this form? 麻煩你填寫這張表格。

32 Please call my hotel as soon as you find it.
尋獲的話，請盡速打電話到飯店與我聯絡。

4 遺失護照 🎧115

33 I've lost my passport. 我的護照掉了。

34 I left my passport somewhere. 我不知道護照丟到哪裡了。

35 I'd like to report a lost passport.
我的護照遺失了，我想報案。

36 What papers do I need to get a new passport?
申請新護照需要準備哪些文件？

37 Where is the Taiwanese Embassy [Taiwanese Consulate]?
台灣大使館〔台灣領事館〕在哪裡？

38 Can you give me the telephone number of the Taiwanese Embassy? 你可以幫我查台灣大使館的電話號碼嗎？

REISSUE
申請補辦

在國外旅遊，如果物品遭竊或遺失，都是一件掃興的事。但如果不幸發生，該如何將損失降到最低呢？

在出國之前，先影印所有文件，一份留給家人，一份隨身攜帶，但要與正本分開。如此一來，萬一不幸遇到什麼事情，就能將不便的程度減到最低。以下介紹幾種貴重物品遺失時的補辦手續。

遺失護照

先到警察局辦理「失竊證明」（Report of Theft）或是「遺失證明」（Report of Loss），這樣就不用擔心有人冒用身分。

之後，再憑證明文件至本國駐外大使館或代表處補辦護照。

如果出發前準備好護照影本，就可以省去多項手續。

遺失旅行支票

旅行支票的購票證明最好與正本分開存放，並記下支票號碼。

如果有購票證明或支票號碼，到銀行時將可直接申請補發，甚至只需要一通電話即可完成手續，並在短時間內取得補發的支票。

遺失信用卡

為避免信用卡遭盜刷，最好能立即通知發卡銀行，要求停卡或是掛失。

某些發卡銀行甚至可以在短時間內補發新卡，並送至你手上。

遺失機票

須立即通知航空公司，告知班機時間等資料。

大部分航空公司很少能立即補發臨時機票，而是要求旅客先買另一張機票，並將原機票作廢，日後再退還原機票的款項。

39 What's the telephone number for the Taiwanese Embassy? 台灣大使館的電話號碼是幾號？

40 I lost my traveler's checks. 我的旅行支票掉了。

41 These are the check numbers. 這是支票的號碼。

42 Where should I apply for reissue?
重新申請要在哪裡辦手續？

43 Can you reissue them? 可以重新申請嗎？

44 Here is the purchase agreement. 這是購買證明。

45 How long does it take to have them reissued?
重新申請要花多久時間？

46 I've lost my credit card. 我的信用卡掉了。

47 Can you cancel my card number, please?
我要將信用卡作廢。

48 I'd like to get a new card. 我要申請新的信用卡。

5 請求幫助 🎧116

49 Help! 救命啊！

50 Police! 警察！

51 Thief! 小偷啊！

52 Robber! 搶劫啊！

53 Stop him! 抓住他！

54 A man is following me! 有個男人一直跟著我！

55 Fire! 失火了啊！

56 Call the police! 快報警啊！

57 Call an ambulance! 叫救護車！

58 Operator, get me the fire station! 總機，幫我接消防隊！

國人在海外遭遇急難時，如何尋求駐外館處協助？

我國於世界各地共設有一百多個駐外單位，均設置有「急難救助專線電話」，國人於海外需要駐外館處協助時，請於上班時間逕撥最近駐外館處辦公室電話，非上班時間則請撥急難救助專線電話或行動電話。

駐外館處地址、電話和急難救助專線電話，均載於外交部「中華民國駐外館處緊急聯絡電話暨通訊錄」，該通訊錄於機場出境大廳或服務台及本局與分支機構大廳，均可免費取用，亦可於外交部網站「駐外館處」項下查詢。

此外，國內親友也可直接與「外交部緊急聯絡中心」聯繫，電話為0800-085-095，該中心 24 小時服務。

一般護照遺失或被竊案件，請先向當地警察局報案並取得報案證明。通常，駐外館處僅能在上班時間，依據報案證明，補辦護照或核發返國旅行文件。

駐外館處提供旅外國人服務事項，可參閱「中華民國駐外館處提供旅外國人服務項目」。

此外，外交部領事事務局亦編有「出國旅行安全實用手冊」，該小冊同樣可於機場出境大廳或服務台及本局與分支機構大廳免費取得，官網也有提供電子檔供民眾下載，建議出國時隨身攜帶，以備不時之需。

59 I had a traffic accident. 我發生車禍了。

60 Someone's been injured. 有人受傷了。

61 My friend is seriously injured! 我的朋友傷得很嚴重。

62 Please send an ambulance! 請派一輛救護車過來！

63 Where is the telephone booth? 哪裡有公用電話？

64 Can you take me to a hospital? 可以帶我去醫院嗎？

65 I was within the speed limit. 我是在速限內。

66 The other car suddenly changed lanes. 對方突然變換車道。

67 It wasn't my fault. 這不是我的過失。

68 Please give me a copy of the accident report.
請給我車禍證明書。

69 I'm insured against the accident. 我有投保意外險。

collision 碰撞

rear-end collision 尾端衝撞

chain collision 連環車禍

serious injury 重傷

slight injury 輕傷

外交部
緊急聯絡
中心

為加強提供國人旅外急難服務，成立「外交部緊急聯絡中心」，24 小時全年無休，電話為：

國內免付費　0800-085-095（諧音：您幫我‧您救我）
海外付費　　（當地國的國際碼）+886-800-085-095

國人在海外遭遇緊急危難時，可透過該專線電話尋求聯繫協助。非涉及海外急難救助事項，切勿撥打該專線電話，以免線路過度負載，耽誤海外緊急事故處理時效。

倘有護照、簽證及文件證明等問題，請於上班時間撥打外交部領事事務局，總機電話：(02) 2343-2888

外交部一般業務查詢，請於上班時間撥打外交部，總機電話：(02) 2348-2999

中心另設有「旅外國人急難救助全球免付費專線」，目前可適用歐、美、日、韓、澳洲等 22 個國家或地區，電話為：800-0885-0885（諧音：您幫幫我、您幫幫我）

中國大陸地區請撥打「海基會緊急服務專線」，電話為：(02) 2533-9995；香港地區請撥打「陸委會香港辦事處緊急聯絡電話」，電話為：+852-6143-9012 或 +852-9314-0130

說著英語去旅行

二版

作　　者	Carlos Campbell
審　　訂	Judy Majewski
校　　對	陳慧莉
編　　輯	賴祖兒 / 黃鈺云
主　　編	丁宥暄
內文排版	林書玉
封面設計	林書玉
製程管理	洪巧玲
發 行 人	周均亮
出 版 者	寂天文化事業股份有限公司
電　　話	+886-(0)2-2365-9739
傳　　真	+886-(0)2-2365-9835
網　　址	www.icosmos.com.tw
讀者服務	onlineservice@icosmos.com.tw
出版日期	2019 年 12 月 二版一刷

版權所有　請勿翻印

郵撥帳號 1998620-0 寂天文化事業股份有限公司
劃撥金額 600 元（含）以上者，郵資免費。
訂購金額 600 元以下者，請外加郵資 65 元。
〔若有破損，請寄回更換，謝謝。〕

國家圖書館出版品預行編目 (CIP) 資料

說著英語去旅行 / Carlos Campbell 著. --
二版 . -- [臺北市]：寂天文化, 2019.12
　　面；　公分
ISBN 978-986-318-864-3(平裝附光碟片)

1. 英語 2. 旅遊 3. 會話

805.188　　　　　　　　　108019931